THE WORLD'S CLASSICS

563

A HERO OF
OUR OWN TIMES

Oxford University Press, Amen House, London E.C.4

GLASGOW NEW YORK TORONTO MELBOURNE WELLINGTON
BOMBAY CALCUTTA MADRAS KARACHI KUALA LUMPUR
CAPE TOWN IBADAN NAIROBI ACCRA

Mikhail Yurevich Lermontov

A HERO OF OUR OWN TIMES

Translated from the Russian
by
EDEN AND CEDAR PAUL

With an Introduction
by
SIR MAURICE BOWRA

LONDON
OXFORD UNIVERSITY PRESS
NEW YORK TORONTO
1958

MIKHAIL YUREVICH LERMONTOV
Born: Moscow, 3 October 1814
Died: near Piatigorsk, 15 July 1841

A Hero of Our Own Times, *first published in* 1840, *was included in* The World's Classics *in* 1958

PRINTED IN GREAT BRITAIN
AT THE UNIVERSITY PRESS, OXFORD
BY CHARLES BATEY, PRINTER TO THE UNIVERSITY

CONTENTS

INTRODUCTION *by* SIR MAURICE BOWRA	vii
AUTHOR'S INTRODUCTION	xvii
BELA	1
MAKSIM MAKSIMICH	73
PECHORIN'S DIARY	95
PREFACE	97
TAMAN	99
PRINCESS MARY	125
A FATALIST	265

INTRODUCTION

WHEN Lermontov called his five stories *A Hero of Our Own Times*, he meant the title to be taken seriously as a guide to his chief character. Pechorin is in his own way quite as representative of a phase of Russian life as Gogol's Chichikov or Goncharov's Oblomov. It is easy to take him as a portrait of Lermontov himself, and Lermontov has certainly put something of himself into him, notably in the self-analysis which is made with such skill and penetration in *Princess Mary*. But Lermontov knew what he was doing and in his Author's Introduction stated his aim:

The Hero of Our Own Times, gentle reader, is a portrait, but not of one person alone. My Hero embodies the vices of our whole generation in the full flush of development.

From his own experience Lermontov created a living character, who was also typical of his generation, and this generation was one which felt itself so defeated and frustrated that it turned against itself and created havoc and destruction around it. This state of mind was a special Russian development of the Byronism

INTRODUCTION

which swept all Europe. It combined an external misanthropy with hidden longings for affection and tenderness, a cynical estimate of human nature with an admiration for its high, heroic moments, a pursuit of love with a tragic inability to be faithful to it when it came. It was at war both with society and with itself, but just as political tyranny meant that its political or humanitarian ambitions were doomed to failure, so its own inner conflicts found no solution except in an extension to wider fields of chaos and devastation. Lermontov's own life was indeed that of a Byronic hero, without the consolations or the security which enabled Byron to survive. His exiles were not voluntary but enforced, the punishment for his own difficult temperament; he quarrelled not only with enemies but with friends; his death in a duel, at the age of twenty-seven, was, if not actually sought, certainly foreseen and not resisted. The boredom with which Byron made such play and which he managed so skilfully, destroyed Lermontov. His distaste for the society into which he was born was a canker which ate into his being and ruined his happiness. When he saw it as the disease of a whole generation he was not far wrong. The police-state of Nicholas I, which had already ruined Pushkin's life, forbade all

INTRODUCTION

the high romantic aspirations which had come too late to Russia from the French Revolution, and offered in their place the routine of military life with its trivial social pleasures and its violent relaxations in camp and barrack-room. When the Russians absorb a new outlook from western Europe, they tend to develop it with a passionate consistency which is all their own and to transform it into something far more dominating and formidable. So the Byronic irony, which had in it a saving element of unreality, was taken over with complete seriousness, and brought into the open certain dangerous and intractable forces which were already at work in the Russian soul.

Though Lermontov's actual career looks like a series of disasters, he was in fact saved by his genius which enabled him to turn his conflicts into art. In this he was helped, like Pushkin before him, by being exiled to the Caucasus. In the stupendous landscape of mountains and rivers and forests he found a peace which he could never find in St. Petersburg or in the Russian plains, and this enabled him to mature his mastery of words and to give a satisfying form to the tumult of his emotions. To his prose, as to his poetry, he gave a concentrated, critical attention, which was the antithesis of his care-

INTRODUCTION

less disregard for his own ordinary activities. He was remarkably without vanity, and worked only for his own ideal of what a work of art ought to be, and he was mercilessly hard on himself. Though his writing was done in odd moments of campaigns and military duties, he never slackened his grip upon it or passed anything that he did not think to be the best that he could do. His style, so clear and firm and concise, may owe something to Pushkin, but it has a greater freedom of movement and a keener eye for visual effects. He never published a book until he was certain that it really did what he wished it to do, and *A Hero of Our Own Times* reveals what he thought the Russian language ought to be when it turned to narrative. In it there is nothing shapeless or otiose, nothing that we can disregard without missing something in his intention. Byron may have regarded his writing as a mere diversion in a life of action, but Lermontov, who, as a soldier, was brave to the point of recklessness, never thought that the life of action mattered except as material to be turned into words.

It was because his art meant so much to him that Lermontov was able to give to his experiences an objective, independent form. Though he was only twenty-five when he wrote *A Hero*

INTRODUCTION

of Our Own Times, and though he had his full share of the subjectivity which is characteristic of the romantic cult of the self, he transformed it into a detached, self-sufficient art, in which each character has his own full degree of reality and the natural scene is sketched in bold and brilliant lines as something which really lives in its own right and forms a stage and a background for the doings of men. Lermontov may never have felt any temptations to apply the 'pathetic fallacy' to nature, but if he did, he resisted them triumphantly. He loved it entirely for its own sake, not as an extension of himself, and he marked it both in its majestic vastness and its significant details, without making any concessions to conventional views of beauty or to romantic desires for escape. He knows exactly what a journey over mountains in a snowstorm means, what perils untamed nature holds for the soldier or the brigand, how inhuman even the most beautiful scene is in the presence of human passions. So too, though the Caucasus brought him into contact with wild tribesmen very unlike his own companions, and though he marked their songs and their finery, their taste for horses and for women, he neither idealized them as noble savages nor despised them for their lack of civilized virtues. He saw them with a remark-

INTRODUCTION

able detachment as they really were, in their violence and their cunning, their display and their squalor, their passions and their acceptance of defeat. We cannot say whether he liked or admired them. He presents them in their convincing reality and leaves us to form our own opinion of them. However much he disliked his own society, he never deluded himself into thinking that he would be more at home in another, no matter how different.

Even with his own society he shows the same detachment. The Russian officers of his story are presented without malice, even perhaps with affection, though it is an affection tempered by an inflexible determination to shirk nothing important in them. Grushnitsky in *Princess Mary* is in some ways rather absurd, but he is not without pathos in his poses and his longings, and though his death is related in a mood of cold-blooded carelessness as befits the man who has killed him, there is no doubt of its tragic character. The blind boy in *Taman* might easily have been made more sympathetic, but Lermontov knows what such a physical deficiency may mean and does not shirk it. Even when he comes to something much more intimately related to his own life, like Vera, he does indeed portray her from inside, but he makes her live

INTRODUCTION

in her own being and not as an image in the mind of the man whom she loves. His understanding of human character is matched by a determination to let it speak for itself, to make its impression on us through characteristic, revealing words and actions, to play its part in a living world, where everyone has his own unique individuality and conflicts and contradictions.

Though *A Hero of Our Own Times* is built of five separate stories, each of which is complete in itself and has its own shape and temper, yet the whole is more than the sum of the parts. Lermontov carefully builds up his portrait of the central character Pechorin, prepares his way to his climax, and then provides an epilogue to it. In *Bela* Pechorin is introduced only by hearsay. We see him as an old companion has known him, and our curiosity is aroused but left unsatisfied. In *Maksim Maksimich* he himself appears, and we know him as another onlooker sees him. As such he is still enigmatic and a little forbidding. His disdain of an old friend leaves an unpleasant impression, and of course it is meant to do so. The problem has been set, and we are forced to ask what kind of man this really is who acts in so unaccountable a way. In *Taman* we begin to see him from the inside in his own words, but the picture is still kept deliberately incomplete. He gives himself away only up to a point. His sudden response to passion and no less sudden revulsion from it, his streak of brutality and his touch of self-pity, are all in character, but the centre of his being is still left dark. Then in *Princess Mary* we see him in the full range of his nature. Just because he is very intelligent and watches himself with a detached, ironical eye, he spares us nothing about himself. The contradictions and the conflicts of his personality are presented with so unflinching a truth that he emerges as a true son of his time and his circumstances, and Lermontov is justified in the claims which he makes for him. The pointless, brutal duel with Grushnitsky was indeed the kind of thing that happened to Lermontov himself and the actual death is a remarkable forecast of his own. But there is no need to think that he had second sight. Like Pushkin, he lived in a world where duels were common enough affairs and any sensitive, outspoken man might be called to fight one any day. What counts is the climax which the duel brings in the presentation of Pechorin. In it he shows himself as a man who, despite all his gifts, is almost unfit and unable to live with other men, and his departure for a remote fortress is the

INTRODUCTION

right end for him. *A Fatalist* is an epilogue, which almost draws a moral. In its short space it raises the question whether men are foredoomed to a certain end, and though it leaves the question without any clear answer, it expresses a mood which suggests that they are and that there is no escape for them. That Lermontov believed this we can hardly doubt. It was part of his conviction that he was trapped in a way of life from which he could not escape and that the destructive powers which he could not control in himself were part of a wider scheme which would in the end destroy him.

A Hero of Our Own Times presents what is essentially a tragic theme. Pechorin, who has many gifts and even virtues, is ruined by himself. The full horror of his corruption emerges in his dealings with Grushnitsky and the cold-blooded carelessness with which he kills him. Yet his treatment of Vera and the young princess is hardly less distressing, and it is clear that Pechorin is by any standards a lost soul. And yet Lermontov reveals his inner being with so gradual and so skilful a hand that we accept each stage as it comes and feel that it is natural and almost inevitable. The whole process is seen from the inside with so fair an insight that we cannot condemn Pechorin; so clearly is he the

INTRODUCTION

victim of his character and the circumstances which have shaped it. Yet equally we hardly pity him. Just because he has hardened himself against the world and formed his own merciless defences against it, he stands outside compassion and evokes only distress. He is indeed a child of a tragic generation. In creating him Lermontov passed in some sense a judgement on himself, and it is the scrupulous candour of this judgement which not only makes *A Hero of Our Own Times* a consummate work of art but redeems Lermontov from the failings which he knew in himself and presented in so courageous and so honest a spirit.

C. M. BOWRA

AUTHOR'S INTRODUCTION

THE 'introduction' to a book may be at one and the same time a prologue and a conclusion, since it serves to explain the work as a whole, and also to answer expected critics. Usually readers are not interested either in the author's moral purpose or in the attacks made on him by the newspapers, and that is why they don't read introductions. This is regrettable, especially in Russia. Our country is still so young and artless that it does not understand a fable which is not explained by a 'moral'. It does not understand jokes, and misses the significance of irony—being, in fact, uneducated. It does not realize that in a decent book and a decent society there is no place for obvious abuse; that latterday enlightenment has discovered a sharper weapon which, though almost invisible, is as deadly as revilement, so that, under the guise of flattery, it can inflict a fatal wound. The Russian public resembles a countryman who, when he overhears a conversation between two diplomats belonging to States that are at feud, is sure that each must be betraying his own land because

AUTHOR'S INTRODUCTION

he continues to use what seem to be friendly terms.

When it first appeared in print in a periodical, this story imposed a severe test upon the credulity of its readers, and even of some experienced literary critics. Joking apart, people took offence because so immoral a man was presented to them as a Hero of Our Own Times. Others roundly declared that the author had drawn a portrait of himself and his friends. This last accusation is threadbare. Russia is a country where even the most fantastic absurdities are ever and again renewed. The most extravagant fairy-tale will hardly avoid being regarded as an attempt to insult some specific individual.

The Hero of Our Own Times, gentle reader, is a portrait, but not of one person alone. My hero embodies the vices of our whole generation in the full flush of development. Perhaps you will assure me that no one can be so bad as that. To which I rejoin that if you actually believe in the possible existence of tragical and romantic evildoers, why should you doubt the reality of Pechorin? If you have a liking for more dreadful and abnormal characters in fiction, why strain against swallowing my hero, also presented in a novel? Is it the truthfulness of

AUTHOR'S INTRODUCTION

the depiction that makes it touch you to the quick?

You may insist that such a picture can do no good to anybody. Patience, dear reader. Please allow me to differ. There are persons who eat so many sweets that they ruin their digestion. They need bitter medicines—sharp truths. Let me beg you, however, not to jump to the conclusion that the author of this book aspires to become a reformer of public morals. God forbid! I found it agreeable to sketch a contemporary as he presented himself to me—and, unfortunately both for him and for you, I have met him too often. The illness has been diagnosed, but goodness alone knows how to cure it!

BELA

BELA

I was posting from Tiflis. The baggage in my cart consisted of one portmanteau, half filled with notes of my Georgian travels. The greater part of these notes, luckily for you, had been lost; but the trunk with the rest of my things, luckily for me, was safe and sound.

The sun was about to dip behind the snowy ridges when I entered the Koyshaursky Valley. The driver, an Ossete, whipped up his horses, for he wanted to reach the pass over Mount Koyshaursky before dark, and he was singing at the top of his voice. It was a glorious place, that valley. Mountains on all sides, inaccessible reddish cliffs, hung with green ivy and crowned with clumps of oriental plane; yellow slopes streaked with ravines; and there, at a great height, the golden fringe of the snows; while below was the Aragva (joined here by another river whose name I cannot recall), thundering forth from a black gorge filled with mist, to become a silver thread which glittered like the scales of a snake's skin.

At the foot of Mount Koyshaursky, we halted close to an inn. Outside was a noisy crowd of about twenty Georgians and mountaineers, while hard by was a train of camels, the caravan having stopped there for the night. I had to hire oxen to pull my cart up that accursed mountain, for it was late and the road was slippery with ice; while the crest of the hill was about a mile farther.

There was nothing else to do. I hired six oxen and a few Ossetes. One of the latter tossed my portmanteau on to his shoulders, while the others shouted lustily at the oxen, ostensibly to encourage the beasts.

Behind my cart came another, drawn by two yoke of oxen, as if it were a mere nothing, though it was heavily laden. This surprised me. At the back marched the owner, smoking a small silver-mounted Kabardian pipe. He wore an officer's tunic without epaulets, and a Circassian fur-cap. He looked about fifty. His face was tanned by long exposure to the Caucasian sun, and his prematurely grizzled moustache was not quite in keeping with his firm step and the vigour of his aspect. I went up to him and nodded a greeting; he silently answered my nod, and puffed out a great cloud of smoke.

'We're fellow-travellers, it seems?'

He nodded once more, still without a word.

'I suppose you're making for Stavropol?'

'That's it; with government stores.'

'Would you mind telling me why two yoke of oxen can easily draw this laden cart of yours, whereas six beasts can hardly get mine, which is empty, up the hill with the aid of all these Ossetes?'

He smiled, and looked at me significantly.

'I guess you're new to the Caucasus?'

'About a year,' I answered.

He smiled once more.

'What of it?' I urged.

'Oh, well, they're frightful rogues, these Asiatics. You fancy they're helping when they shout? The devil take them and their shouting. The oxen understand them perfectly well. You might harness six more yoke to your cart, and the beasts would hardly stir it while the Ossetes went on yelling like that. Disgusting scoundrels. But there's nothing to be done with such fellows. What they like is exorting money from travellers. They're utterly corrupt. You'll see, they'll be asking you for vodka in a minute. I know their little ways. They can't impose upon me.'

'Have you served long in these parts?'

'Yes, I began to serve here in the days of Aleksei Petrovich Ermoloff,' he replied, drawing himself up. 'When the general came to

BELA

take command on the frontier, I was a sub-lieutenant,' he continued, 'and under him I was twice promoted in the affair against the mountaineers.'

'What are you doing now?'

'Now I belong to the third infantry battalion. Why are you travelling in the Caucasus, if I may ask?'

I told him.

With that our conversation came to an end, and we walked side by side in silence. Near the top of the mountain we crossed the snow-line. The sun had set and night followed day almost without pause, as is usual in the south; but thanks to the glimmer from the snow we could easily distinguish the road, which still led uphill, though now less steeply. I gave orders for my portmanteau to be put back into the cart, and for the oxen to be replaced by horses. Then for the last time I looked down into the valley, but a thick fog, pouring out in wave after wave from the gorge, hid it completely, and not a sound rose from it to our ears. The Ossetes flocked round me noisily, demanding vodka, but the captain shouted at them so menacingly that they instantly dispersed.

'What a measly crowd!' he exclaimed. 'They can't ask for bread in Russian, but they've learned how to say: "Officer, give vodka." To my way of thinking, even the Tartars are better; anyhow they don't drink.'

It was nearly another mile to the posting-station. We were surrounded by silence—a silence so intense that from the buzzing of a gnat you could have told which way it was flying. On the left were deep, black clefts; beyond them, in front of us, dark-blue mountain tops, furrowed and wrinkled, covered with snowdrifts, stood out against the pallid skyline, where the light of departing day lingered. In the dark vault of heaven stars had begun to twinkle, and (strangely enough) they seemed to me much higher than the stars I was used to in the north. On both sides of the road there projected bare, black rocks; and here and there, thrusting from beneath the snow, were patches of brushwood; but not a withered leaf stirred, and amid this profoundly sleeping nature it was comforting to hear the snorting of our weary team and the irregular tinkling of its Russian bell.

'We're going to have splendid weather tomorrow,' I said.

The captain did not answer in words, but with his forefinger directed my attention to a high mountain which stood right in front of us.

BELA

'What's that?' I asked.

'Gut-Gora.'

'Well, what of it?'

'Look how it's steaming.'

Indeed Gut-Gora was steaming. Along the flanks of the mountain there crept thin wisps of vapour, but on the top lay a thick, black storm-cloud, so black that it made a blotch upon the dark sky.

By now I could see the posting-station, and the roofs of the huts which clustered round it. Before us shone cheerful little fires. But at this moment a cold, raw wind came roaring through the pass, and fine rain began to fall. I was barely able to wrap myself in my felt cloak before it was snowing heavily, and I looked enquiringly at the captain.

'We shall have to put up here for the night,' he said grumpily. 'No use trying to cross the ridge in this snowstorm.' He turned to my driver. 'What d'you think? Have there been avalanches from Krestovoy?'

'Not yet, Sir,' answered the Ossete, 'but there are plenty just on the point of falling.'

Since the posting-station had no accommodation for travellers, we dossed in a smoke-begrimed Tartar hut. I invited my companion to have a glass of tea with me, having brought a cast-iron teapot along—my sole consolation during my travels in the Caucasus.

One side of the hut was built against the rock. Three wet and slippery steps led up to the door. I groped my way in, and stumbled over a cow (the cowshed with these people takes the place of the servants' hall). I didn't know where to turn, for there were sheep baaing in one direction and dogs yapping in another. A faint gleam of light came from somewhere, and it guided me to another opening that resembled a doorway. Through this there disclosed itself a very remarkable sight. The roomy Tartar hut, whose roof was supported by two smoke-begrimed pillars, was full of people. In the middle crackled a wood fire, established on the mud floor, and the smoke, continually pushed back by gusts of wind from a hole in the roof, spread so thick a shroud in the interior that it was difficult to distinguish anything. At the fire were sitting two old women, a herd of children, and one skinny Georgian—all in rags. We had to make the best of it. I squatted by the fire, lit a pipe, and soon the teapot began to sing merrily.

'Poor wretches,' I said to the captain, pointing at our hosts, who were filthy, and stared at us without a word, as if petrified.

'As stupid as they make them,' he answered.

BELA

'Would you believe it? They can do absolutely nothing, and it is impossible to teach them. If only they were Kabardians or Chechens, who, though robbers and rogues, are at any rate desperate blades; but these chaps have no weapons even for hunting; you won't find as much as one decent dagger among them. They're typical Ossetes.'

'Were you long among the Chechens?'

'Oh, yes, ten years. I was stationed with my company at Kamenny Fort. Know it?'

'I've heard of it.'

'Well, old man, they were cutthroats there, if you like! Now, thanks be, the times are peaceful; but I've seen the days when, if you went a hundred paces outside the walls you'd come across a shaggy devil on watch, and you had to keep your eyes skinned if you didn't want to get a lasso round your neck or a bullet in the back of your head. Fine fellows, they were.'

'I suppose you had some strange adventures?' I said, curiosity stirring.

'What else could you expect?'

He began to tug at the left side of his moustache, bent his head forward, and plunged into thought. I was eager to get a yarn out of him, this desire being natural in a traveller and a man of letters. The tea was ready. Taking two glasses out of my portmanteau, I filled them from the teapot and put one of them in front of him. He sipped, and went on as if talking to himself:

'Yes, I had some strange adventures.'

This remark made me feel hopeful. I knew that old campaigners in the Caucasus were fond of spinning yarns, when they got an opportunity, which was seldom, for they would often spend as much as five years at a stretch on service in some lonely spot without ever being greeted by a stranger. The only conversation they heard at the mess-table concerned the savagery of the natives; the risks of everyday life. But strange things happen to them and it is a pity so few of them write.

'Wouldn't you like a dash of rum in your tea?' I asked my companion. 'I brought some white rum with me from Tiflis—and it's very cold here.'

'Many thanks, but I never touch spirits.'

'Why is that?'

'Just because . . . I took the pledge. When I was still only a sub-lieutenant, at the mess one evening we all got a little screwed. Then came news of a threatened attack, and we were half-seas-over when we went on duty. We never found out how it came to Aleksei Petrovich's ears; but good God, there was a hell of a row.

He nearly had us court-martialled. That's the way things turn out. You live a year and nothing goes wrong; but if you happen to have had too much vodka, as likely as not you'll be reported and broken.'

He was straying from the point, and I nearly lost hope.

'Look at the Circassians,' he went on. 'The way they swill that heavy beer of theirs, at a wedding or a funeral, makes them fighting-mad. I barely escaped with my life once, when I went to a party given by a friendly chief.'

'How did it happen?'

'Like this.' He filled his pipe, took a draw, and began his story. 'Nearly five years ago I was stationed in the fortress on the other side of the Terek with my company. One day in the autumn a food-transport arrived, in charge of a young officer who was about twenty-five. Presenting himself to me in parade uniform, he told me that he had been assigned to the fortress. He was thin and pale but spick-and-span, and his rig-out was so immaculate, that I could see he was new to the Caucasus.

'"I suppose you've just been transferred from Russia?" I asked.

'"Yes, Captain, that's so," he answered.

'Shaking hands, I said:

BELA

'"Very glad to make your acquaintance. 'Fraid you'll find it rather dull here. But I'm sure we shall get on well together. Drop titles, won't you? Call me plain Maksim Maksimich. And you needn't bother to turn up always in full kit. We wear undress uniform most of the time."

'I showed him his quarters, and he settled in.'

'What was his name?' I asked Maksim Maksimich.

'His name? Oh, Gregory Aleksandrovich Pechorin. He was a good fellow, but a bit queer, all the same. For instance, when it was raining in torrents, or very cold, he would go out shooting for the whole day, regardless. The rest of us would be chilled to the bone, or get dog-tired; but not he. Another time one would be sitting with him in his room when the wind was blowing, and he would swear he would get a chill; or if the shutters rattled, he would tremble and turn pale. Yet when we were out after boar, he would face up to the tuskers like anything. Sometimes for a whole hour one couldn't get a word out of him; then suddenly he would begin to talk, and would make you split your sides with laughter. Yes, he was a strange fellow; a rich man, too—had lots of expensive things.'

'How long did he stay with you?' I enquired.

'About a year. I shan't forget that year in a hurry. It brought me trouble; but no matter. Indeed, there are persons concerning whom it is written from birth that those who become associated with them shall have extraordinary experiences.'

'Extraordinary?' I interjected, with curiosity, pouring him out some more tea.

'I'll tell you. Four miles from our fortress, lived a friendly Circassian chieftain. His son, a youngster of fifteen, had a habit of coming to see us, almost every day, now on one pretext, now on another. Gregory Aleksandrovich used to spoil him, and so did the rest of us. But he was the greatest ruffian you can imagine, besides being skilful and quick-witted; he could pick up a cap from the ground while riding at full gallop, and was a splendid marksman. His weak point was, his greed for money. Once, for a lark, Gregory Aleksandrovich promised to give him a chervonets if he could steal the best billy-goat from his father's herd. Well, would you believe it, the very next night he lugged the beast here by the horns. Fierce, too. If we ever took it into our heads to tease him, his eyes would flash, and he would put his hand on the hilt of his dagger.

'"Look out, Azamat," I would say to him,

"don't get your dander up, or someone will slit your weazand for you."

'Well, a day came when the old chieftain, the father, invited us to a wedding. He was marrying off his eldest daughter, and nothing would suit him but that we should come along as guests. It wouldn't do, of course, to refuse such an invitation from friendly Tartars; so we set out for the party. When we got to the village, a lot of dogs rushed out at us, making a great to-do. At sight of us, the women went into hiding, except for a few, who allowed us to see their faces, and were anything but beautiful.

'"I had a much better opinion of the Circassian women's looks," said Gregory Aleksandrovich.

'"Wait a bit," I answered with a smile—for I had something up my sleeve.

'Many people had already assembled in the chief's hut. Among Asiatics, you know, it's the custom to use a small-meshed net when sending invitations to a wedding. But they welcomed us with all the honours, and conducted us into the guest-chamber. However, I did not forget to notice where they stabled our horses, since it was well to be prepared for all emergencies.'

'Do they make a great fuss about their weddings?' I asked the captain.

'As a rule. To begin with, the mullah reads some passages from the Koran; then they give presents to the young couple and all the relatives; these come and drink vast quantities of beer; soon it's time for the display of horsemanship; and always some ragamuffin or other, mounted on a sorry screw, makes grimaces, plays the clown, amuses the honourable company; after nightfall, there begins a dance—of sorts. A poor old buffer strums on the three-stringed—oh, I've forgotten what they call it—something like our balalaïka. The girls and the boys stand in two rows, facing one another, clap their hands and sing. Then a girl and a woman walk down the middle intoning to one another, verses, improvising, whatever comes into their heads, while the others join in the chorus. This evening Pechorin and I were sitting in the place of honour when there came up to us our host's younger daughter, a girl of sixteen, and started singing—how shall I put it?—compliments to my companion,'

'Can you remember exactly what she sang?'

'This sort of thing: "Well-built, they say, are our young crack-riders, and their caftans are trimmed with silver; but the young Russian officer is more shapely than they are, and his tunic is braided with gold. He is like a poplar when

BELA

compared with them; for such poplars do not grow, cannot flourish, in our fields."

'Pechorin stood up, bowed to her, raised his hand to his forehead and his heart, and begged me to answer her. I can speak their lingo fluently, and I translated what he said.

'When she had gone away, I whispered to Gregory Aleksandrovich:

'"Well, what do you think of her?"

'"Charming," he answered. "Do you know her name?"

'"Bela," I replied.

'Indeed, she was beyond praise. She was tall and slender, her eyes were as dark as those of a chamois, and she seemed to gaze into one's very soul. Pechorin was so profoundly impressed that he couldn't keep from watching her, and she continued to look at him on the sly. But it was not only Pechorin who was smitten by the pretty little princess. From a corner of the room someone else stared at her ardently, with a fixed and burning glance. I kept close watch, for I knew my old acquaintance Kazbich. He was an odd fish who could not be precisely classified either as friend or foe. A good deal of suspicion attached to him, but no definite misdeed had ever been proved against him. From time to time he brought sheep to us in the fortress, and sold them for very little, without haggling. He just stated his price, and you had to take it or leave it; wouldn't have abated a farthing if you had put a knife to his throat. It was said that he liked to hobnob with the brigands on the other side of the Kuban. Certainly his phiz suggested that he was a robber; a little fellow, and lean, but broad-shouldered, and as crafty as the devil. His clothes were old, torn, and patched, but his weapons were silver-mounted. As for his horse, it was famous throughout Kabarda, for indeed you couldn't dream of a more splendid creature. Other horsemen had good reason for envying Kazbich the treasure, and many had tried to steal him; but in vain. I can picture the animal even now: black as pitch, slender-limbed, eyes as lovely as Bela's. Amazingly strong, with plenty of go in him after a thirty-mile gallop; knew his rider's voice, and would come like a dog when called. No need to hitch him anywhere. Perfect animal for a robber.

'That evening Kazbich was as sullen as could be, and I noticed that beneath his outer garment he was wearing chain-mail. "There's a reason for that," I thought. "He's up to some game or other."

'It was stifling indoors, and I went out for a

BELA

breath of fresh air. Night was falling, and mists were gathering on the passes.

'The fancy took me to visit the shed where our horses were stabled, for I wanted to see that they had fodder, and it would be as well to make sure that they had come to no harm. My own horse was a fine one, as every Kabardian who saw him said admiringly in the Tartar tongue. I was making my way quietly along the fence, when suddenly I heard voices. One of them I instantly recognized as that of the young scamp Azamat, the chieftain's son; his companion's I did not know—someone speaking in low tones. What were they colloguing about? My horse? I crouched by the rails listening, for I didn't want to miss a word. But now and again the noise of singing and chatter from the company inside would drown the murmur of this interesting conversation. Still, I heard a good deal.

'"You've a magnificent horse," said Azamat. "If I were master here and had a drove of three hundred brood mares, I'd give half of them for that galloper of yours, Kazbich."

'"Kazbich," I thought, remembering the chain-mail.

'"Yes," answered Kazbich, after a brief silence, "in all Kabardia you wouldn't find such another. Once—it was on the farther side of the Terek—I went with the brigands to capture some Russian droves, but we muffed it, and had to scatter in all directions. Four Cossacks chased me. I could hear the shouts of the giaours, and in front of me there was a thick wood. Crouching low in the saddle, I commended myself to Allah, and for the first time in my life insulted the stallion by using my whip. Like a bird he sped among the branches; sharp thorns tore my clothes, and the dry twigs of the cork-oaks lashed me in the face. The horse leapt over tree-stumps and gallantly breasted the undergrowth. I should have done better to dismount, leave him outside, and seek a hiding-place in the wood on foot, but I couldn't bear to part from him—and in the end the Prophet rewarded me. Bullets whistled past my head, and I could hear the hurrying Cossacks close on my trail. Unexpectedly a deep ravine appeared in front of me; my mount gathered himself together, and jumped. His rear hoofs failed to reach the opposite bank, to which he clung only by his forelegs. Letting go the reins, I dropped into the gully. This saved my horse, for he was able to scramble up. The Cossacks had seen everything but they did not trouble to look for me in the ravine, thinking, no doubt, that I had been dashed to pieces, and I could hear them as they thundered past, trying to catch the horse. My heart bled. I had fallen (without worse injury than a shaking) on to leaves and thick grass at the bottom of the gorge, which was not very deep. Looking down it, I could see the end of the wood. There were some Cossacks in the open; so was my black beauty, Karagyoz, galloping straight towards them. They all made for him, shouting like mad. He wheeled to avoid them; they surrounded and chivvied him; and two of them almost succeeded in lassoing him by the neck. Trembling, I turned away my eyes and began to pray. But in a few moments I looked once more—to see Karagyoz speeding freely into the distance, his tail streaming in the wind, while the giaours, pursuing him across the steppe on their tired horses, were far behind, and stretched out into a long line. By God, it's true; absolutely true. Till late that night I sat unheeded in the gully. Then, what do you think, Azamat? In the darkness, I heard something. A horse's hoofs upon the bank of the ravine; a horse that snorted, whinnied, pawed the ground. I recognized the neighing of my Karagyoz, my comrade. Since then, nothing can part us."

'I could plainly hear him fondling the stallion's

glossy neck, and murmuring terms of endearment.

'"If I had a drove of a thousand brood mares," said Azamat, "I would give them all in exchange for your Karagyoz."

'"No go, my lad; nothing doing," answered Kazbich carelessly.

'"I have been told, Kazbich," said Azamat in a wheedling tone, "that you're a fine fellow, a crack rider. Now my father is afraid of the Russians, and won't let me go into the mountains. Give me your horse, and I'll do anything you want. I'll steal for you my father's best carbine or scimitar, anything you have a fancy for. The scimitar he's wearing today is of famous make. Touch your arm with the edge and you'll find out. A coat of mail like yours is no defence against a blade such as that."

'Kazbich made no answer.

'"The first time I saw that horse of yours," went on Azamat, "watched him curvetting with you astride, jumping with dilated nostrils, noticed the pebbles scatter from beneath his hoofs, something strange happened inside me, and since then I've lost interest in everything else. I look at my father's best horses with contempt, would be ashamed to be seen riding one of them. I'm sick with longing. I sit on the top of the cliff thinking all the time of that coal-black stallion of yours with his marvellous paces, his shining coat, his spine straight as an arrow. He seems to present himself before me with his fiery eyes—oh, I can find no words to express what I feel. I shall die, Kazbich, if you won't sell him to me," concluded Azamat, his voice trembling with passion.

'He burst into tears. Azamat was a stout-hearted youngster, and it took a good deal to make him cry, even when he was much younger.

'The answer to his weeping was something in the nature of a chuckle.

'"I hear you laughing at me," said Azamat, now in a steady voice. "Well, you shall see I'm ready to risk anything. Do you want me to steal my sister for you? How she dances! How she sings! Her gold embroideries are a perfect marvel. Not all the padishahs of Turkey have ever had such a woman in their harems. Do you want her? Wait for me tomorrow night, in the gorge, by the stream, just beyond the last hamlet. I will bring her, and she will be yours. Isn't Bela worth as much as your stallion?"

'There was a long silence. Then, instead of giving a direct answer, Kazbich hummed the words of an old song.

BELA

'"Beautiful maidens abound in your home,
Shining their eyes and sweet with them to roam,
Maddening their kisses, to love them a joy—
Better is freedom than love's fragile toy.

'"Women have prices we reckon in gold.
Horses, I tell you, have value untold.
Not the wind on the steppe is so swift as my steed.—
He disappoints not, nor makes my heart bleed."

'Vainly did Azamat plead with him, weep, flatter, cozen, utter many vows. It was to no purpose. At length Kazbich cut him short impatiently, saying:

'"Clear out, you senseless brat. What would you do with my stallion? He would throw you after three paces, and you'd break your neck on the stones."

'"Throw me!" shouted Azamat in a fury, and the point of the boy's dagger clinked upon the man's coat of mail.

'A powerful hand thrust the youngster away, hurling him against the wall of the shed with so much violence that it rattled with the shock.

'"There'll be a fine row," thought I, hurrying into the stable, where I bridled our horses, and led them out into the back yard. Within two minutes, the Tartar headquarters were in an uproar. This is what happened. Azamat rushed in with his clothing torn, and declared that Kazbich had tried to murder him. General exodus; arms in everyone's hands, and the devil to pay. Vociferations and gunshots. Kazbich was already in the saddle prancing about amid the crowd in the street, brandishing his scimitar, and looking like a perfect fiend.

'"This is a bad business, getting mixed up in other people's troubles," I said to Gregory Aleksandrovich, taking him by the hand. "Don't you think we'd better make ourselves scarce as quick as we can?"

'"Oh, let's wait and see it through," he answered.

'"I know it will end in disaster. That's the way with these Asiatics; when they get full of beer, the slaughter begins."

'So we mounted, and galloped off home.'

'But what happened to Kazbich?' I asked the captain eagerly.

'A row is a trifle to people of that sort,' he answered finishing his glass of tea. 'Kazbich just slipped away.'

'Wasn't he wounded?'

'God knows. A robber has nine lives, like a cat. I've seen some of them at work, cut all to pieces, riddled like a sieve with bayonet wounds, but they go on using their swords as if there were nothing the matter.'

After a brief silence the captain resumed, stamping irritably on the floor: 'One thing I shall never forgive myself. I suppose the devil tempted me. On our way back to the fortress I told Gregory Aleksandrovich what I had heard while I crouched by the fence. Laughing to himself, he went into a brown study. He'd formed a plan.'

'What was it all about? Please tell me.'

The captain had to go on with his tale.

'In about four days Azamat turned up at the fortress. As usual, he came to see Gregory Aleksandrovich, whose habit it was to give him sweetmeats. I was there. The conversation turned upon horses, and Pechorin began to talk about Kazbich's stallion: how spirited he was, how lovely, as graceful as a chamois—in a word, there wasn't another horse like him in the whole world. The young Tartar's eyes glistened, but Pechorin pretended not to notice. I spoke of other things, but the boy continually brought the conversation back to Kazbich's galloper.

'It was the same whenever Azamat came to visit us. About three weeks afterwards, I noticed that the youngster was growing pale and had lost flesh, like a love-sick man in a novel. What a strange thing. But later I learned the whole story. Gregory Aleksandrovich was deliberately tormenting him, to make him ready for anything, saying, for instance:

"'I can see, Azamat, what a fancy you have taken for that horse, but you seem about as likely to get him as to see the nape of your own neck. Well, tell me what you would give me if I were to make you a present of him?"

"'Anything you like, anything in the world,' replied Azamat.

"'In that case, I'll get him for you, upon one condition. Swear to fulfil it."

"'I'll swear all right. But you must swear too."

"'Well and good. I promise you shall have the stallion; but in return you must give me your sister Bela. Karagyoz will be her price. I hope you think you're making a good bargain."

'Azamat said nothing.

"'You don't like it? As you please. I thought you were grown up, but I see you're still only a child. You don't really care yet about riding."

'Azamat could hardly contain himself.

"'But what about my father?" he said.

"'Doesn't he go away sometimes?"

"'True . . . but . . ."

"'Is it a bargain?"

"'It's a bargain,'" whispered Azamat, pale as death. "When?"

"'The next time Kazbich comes here. He's

BELA

promised to let us have a dozen sheep. You can leave the rest to me. Watch out, Azamat."

'That was how they settled the affair, and, to speak frankly, it was a black business. When I said as much afterwards to Pechorin, he only answered that a wild Circassian girl might think herself lucky to get so good a husband as himself—for to their way of thinking he would be Bela's husband, while Kazbich was nothing but a robber for whom any punishment would be less than the rascal's deserts. Judge for yourself what arguments I could put for the other side. But at the moment I did not even know that the bargain had been struck. Kazbich turned up after a while and asked whether we didn't need some sheep and honey. I told him to bring them along next day.

'"Azamat," said Gregory Aleksandrovich, "tomorrow Karagyoz will be in my hands. If Bela is not here tonight, you won't get the stallion."

'"Right you are," answered Azamat, and galloped off home.

'In the evening Gregory Aleksandrovich, fully armed, left the fortress. Just how matters were arranged, I don't know, but at night the pair of them came back, and the sentry noticed that in front of Azamat's saddle lay a woman, tied hand and foot, her head muffled in a thick veil.'

BELA

'But what about Karagyoz?' I asked the captain.

'I'm coming to that in a moment. Early next day Kazbich arrived with a dozen sheep for sale. Having hitched his mount to the fence, he came to my quarters. I ordered some tea, for though the man was a robber, he was my guest all the same.

'We chatted of one thing and another. Suddenly I noticed that Kazbich was trembling, and that his expression had changed. He rushed to the window—which, unfortunately, gave upon the back yard.

'"What's the matter with you?" I asked.

'"My horse, my horse," he said, shuddering all over.

'"Certainly I heard the clatter of hoofs. Some Cossack messenger has arrived."

'"No, it's you accursed Russians," he bellowed, rushing headlong from the room, as savage as a panther.

'With two bounds he was in the open. At the gates of the fortress, the sentry tried to bar his way. He leapt over the man's musket and ran into the road. In the distance was a cloud of dust raised by Azamat galloping off at full speed on Karagyoz. Still running, Kazbich unslung his carbine and fired. Then, for about a minute, he stood motionless, until he was sure that he had missed. Thereupon he began to whimper, banged the carbine against the rocks, breaking it to pieces, flung himself on the ground, and sobbed like a child. The men from the fortress gathered round him; he paid no heed to them. They stood for a while discussing the matter, and then went in. I sent an orderly to pay what was due to him for the sheep. He wouldn't touch the money, but lay face downwards, as still as a corpse. Would you believe it? He stayed like that till late in the night, and indeed the whole night through. Only next morning did he come into the fortress and ask for the name of the kidnapper. The sentry who had seen Azamat unhitch the stallion and gallop off did not think it necessary to make any secret about the matter. When Kazbich heard the name, his eyes glittered, and he went off to the village where Azamat's father was chieftain.'

'What did the father do?' I asked.

'That was the difficulty. Kazbich didn't find him. He'd gone away for a week. Otherwise Azamat wouldn't have been able to carry off Bela.

'When the father got back, neither son nor daughter was there. Azamat was no fool, and quite understood that if he were caught it might cost him his life. He just vanished, and has never been heard of from that day to this. He probably joined some band of marauders. May have got killed on the other side of the Terek or the Kuban. If so, it served him right.

'I must admit that I myself was somewhat to blame. As soon as I learned that the Circassian woman was in Gregory Aleksandrovich's quarters, I put on full regimentals and went to him.

'He was lying on a couch in the outer room, one hand under the back of his neck, holding in the other hand an unlit pipe. The door leading to the inner room was locked, and the key was not in the keyhole. These details struck me at the first glance. I coughed significantly, and clattered my heels on the threshold, but he pretended not to hear.

'"Ensign," I said, as sternly as I could. "Is it possible you're not aware that I've entered your room?"

'"Ah, how d'you do, Maksim Maksimich," he answered, without rising. "Don't you want to smoke?"

'"Excuse me, I'm not simply Maksim Maksimich; you must address me as Captain."

'"Don't bother about that. It makes no difference. Would you like some tea? If you only knew what a lot of worries I've got."

BELA

'"I know everything," I answered, going up to the couch.

'"So much the better. I needn't trouble to tell you."

'"Ensign, you have committed an offence for which I also shall be held responsible."

'"Don't put on side. What are you making a fuss about? You know it's been share and share alike between us for so long."

'"You mustn't try to turn this into a joke. Your sword, please."

'"Mitka, my sword."

'Mitka brought the sword. Having done my duty, I sat down beside Pechorin, and went on:

'"Listen, Gregory Aleksandrovich. Admit that it wasn't right."

'"What wasn't right?"

'"To carry off Bela. Your bargain with that cunning rogue Azamat. Now admit it," I said.

'"But I was so tremendously taken with her."

'What answer could I make to that? The plea left me dumbfounded. Anyhow, after a brief silence, I told him that if Bela's father came to demand her, she would have to be given up.

'"I don't see that for a moment," he answered.

'"Do you think he knows she is here?"

'"How can he know?"

'Again I was stumped.

"'Listen to me, Maksim Maksimich,' said Pechorin, sitting up, 'really you're a good chap, but if you were to give the girl back to her father, who's a savage, he would cut her throat, or sell her. What's done is done. Don't make things out worse than they are. Let the girl stay with me, and give me back my sword.'

"'I'd better see her,' I answered.

"'She's on the other side of that door. But I myself tried just now to have a talk with her, and it was of no use. She's sitting in the corner, huddled up in her shawl; won't answer, and won't look at me. She's as timid as a gazelle. I sent for the woman who keeps the inn here, and can speak Circassian. The good lady was to try and reconcile her to the idea that she was mine, and could not henceforward belong to anyone but me.' He struck his fist on the table, and continued: 'Yes, by God, I'm willing to marry her. . . . Well, what are we going to do about it? There are people whom nothing can make reasonable.'"

'What happened in the end?' I asked Maksim Maksimich. 'Did she accommodate herself to him, or pine away in captivity, perish of home-sickness?'

'Why should she perish of home-sickness? She was able to see from the windows of the fortress the very same mountains she used to see from her native village, and these people are quite happy so long as they can see mountains. Every day Gregory Aleksandrovich brought her a present of some sort. To begin with she silently and proudly spurned his gifts, which thereupon the hostess of the inn appropriated, with much expenditure of eloquence.—Lovely trifles! What will a woman not do for coloured rags? But this by the way.—Gregory Aleksandrovich had a long fight of it. While it was going on, he learned to speak Circassian, and Bela made some progress in understanding Russian. Little by little she got used to looking at him, furtively to begin with, out of the corner of her eyes, while seeming desperately sorrowful, and singing her songs softly, mournfully, so that it touched even me to the quick when I heard her from the next room.

'Never shall I forget one scene which I witnessed when I glanced in on passing the window. Bela was seated with her head bent low, and Gregory Aleksandrovich was standing in front of her. "Listen, my peri," he said. "You must know that sooner or later you will be mine. Why then do you go on torturing me? Is it possible that you are in love with one of your Circassian youths? If so, I will send you home at once." She shuddered almost imperceptibly, and shook her head. Then she sighed. "Or is it your religion which prevents your loving me?" She turned pale, but made no answer. "Believe me, Allah is for all races one and the same, and if it be His will that I should love you, what can forbid you to love me in return?" She looked at him fixedly, as if struck by this new idea. Her expression was diffident, and showed a desire to be convinced. What eyes she had, eyes like stars, like burning coals!

'"Listen to me, Bela darling," went on Pechorin. "You see how much I love you. I would give my head to cheer you. I want you to be happy, and if you begin to pine once more, I shall die of grief. Tell me you will be cheerful." She was thoughtful, and did not turn her dark eyes away. Then she smiled, looked friendly, and nodded as a token of assent. He took her hand, and tried to persuade her to let him kiss her. She resisted weakly, saying again and again: "No, no, please don't." He persisted; she trembled, and burst into tears. "I am your prisoner," she said, "your slave; of course you can kiss me by force if you will."—More tears.

'Gregory Aleksandrovich slapped his own head furiously, and rushed into the outer room. I went in to see him. Wringing his hands, he was striding up and down. "Hullo, old boy, what's the matter?" I enquired.

'"She's a devil, not a woman," he answered; "but I swear to you that she shall be mine."

'I shook my head.

'"Do you want to bet?" he asked. "Within a week. Done?"

'We shook hands, and I went away.

'Next day the whim seized him to send a man to Kizlyar for various purchases. A cartload of them came back; Persian stuffs of one sort and another, too many to specify.

'"What do you think? Maksim Maksimich?" he asked, when he showed me his presents. "Will my Asiatic beauty be able to resist the onslaught of such a battery?"

'"You don't know much about Circassian women," I answered. "They're different from the Georgians, or the Transcaucasian Tartars—utterly different. They have their own peculiar principles, being differently brought up."

'Gregory Aleksandrovich smiled, and began to whistle a march.

'But it turned out that I was right. The presents had very little effect. The prisoner remained friendly and confiding. That was all, so he decided upon a last expedient. One morning he ordered a horse to be saddled, dressed himself as a Circassian (weapons and all), and went to her.

'"Bela," he said, "you know how much I love you. When I made up my mind to carry you off, I thought that as soon as you knew me you would fall in love with me. Well, I made a mistake, so I am going to bid you farewell. You can stay here as absolute mistress of all that I possess, or you can go back to your father, as you like. You are free. I have done you a grievous wrong, and must punish myself as best I can. Good-bye. I am going away. Whither? How can I tell. Maybe I shall go in search of a bullet or a sword-thrust. If that should be my end, remember me and forgive me."

'He turned away, stretching out his hand in farewell. She did not take it, and said nothing.

'I was standing in the doorway, could see her lovely face clearly, and it was most depressing to notice how pale she was.

'Not getting any answer, Pechorin took a few steps towards the door. He was trembling, and I can assure you he seemed to me ready to fulfil in earnest what he had said only as make-believe. That's the sort of fellow he was, but God alone knows the truth of it. However, before he reached the door, she ran up to him sobbing, and flung her arms round his neck.

BELA

Will you believe me that I too, watching from the outer door, almost burst into tears, idiotic as it may seem to you.'

The captain said no more for a little while. Then he went on, pulling at his moustache:

'I can assure you I felt vexed that no woman had ever loved me as that woman loved Pechorin.'

'Were they happy together for a long time?' I asked.

'Yes, indeed. She told us that from the first day on which she saw Gregory Aleksandrovich, he had often appeared to her in her dreams, and that no other man had ever made such an impression on her. Oh, yes, they were happy.'

'How commonplace,' I involuntarily exclaimed.

I had been waiting for a tragical finale—and, after all, my expectations were disappointed.

'Is it possible,' I went on, 'that the father never found out that Bela had been made prisoner in the fortress?'

'He had his suspicions. But within a few days we were told that the old fellow had been killed. This is how it happened.'

I was all attention.

'I must tell you that Kazbich believed Azamat had stolen the horse with the chieftain's connivance. At any rate I suppose so. He lay in wait for the fancied offender one day on the road, about two miles from the village. The old man was returning after a vain search for Bela; his retainers had fallen behind; night was coming on; he rode plunged in thought. Of a sudden Kazbich pounced on him like a cat, rushing out of an ambush in a coppice, leapt on to the horse's back behind him, stabbed him so that he rolled out of the saddle, seized the reins, and was off in a flash. Some of the followers saw it from a mound nearby. Of course they gave chase, but didn't catch the murderer.'

'So he paid himself the price of his horse—and took vengeance,' I said, wishing to sound my companion for his opinion.

'Naturally,' replied the captain; 'and by Tartar standards he was perfectly justified.'

I could not but be struck by this instance of the ready way in which a Russian can adapt himself to the customs of the people among whom he happens to live. I don't know whether this faculty is blameworthy or commendable, but it is a proof of our incomparable suppleness, and of the existence of that clear and sound understanding which enables us to pardon evil when we see its inevitability or the impossibility of averting it.

Meanwhile we had finished our tea. The horses had been harnessed for a long while and stood shivering in the snow. The moon was paling in the west, on the point of sinking behind black storm-clouds which, like fragments of torn curtains, overhung the distant peaks. We went out of the Tartar hut. Notwithstanding my fellow-traveller's forecast, the weather had cleared, and there was promise of a quiet morning. Strangely shaped constellations were outlined upon the far horizon, but were gradually disappearing as in the east a glimmer of dawn fringed the dark-purple dome of the sky, and the steep mountain slopes covered with virgin snows disclosed themselves in the growing dawn. To right and to left hung gloomy, mysterious abysses; while among the interstices of the nearer rocks mist-wreaths crept and writhed like serpents, as if aware of and dreading the approach of day.

Everything was peaceful both in the heavens and on earth, as in a man's heart at the hour of morning prayer; only now and again there blew a cold breeze from the east, ruffling the manes of the horses, which were covered with hoar-frost. We set out. It was hard work for five lean and sorry screws to pull our carts up the winding road to Gut-Gora. We walked behind, shoving stones under the wheels whenever the beasts got winded and had to rest. The road appeared to be leading up into the sky, for it continued to mount as far as the eye could see, and at length vanished into the cloud which had stayed since overnight upon the summit of Gut-Gora like a kite hovering over its prey. The snow crunched beneath our feet. The air was so rarefied that breathing was painful, and the blood continually went to my head; but, for all that, a delightful feeling of exhilaration spread through my veins, and I was full of joy at being, as it were, on the roof of the world—a childish sentiment, no doubt, but when we get right away from the conventions of society and close to nature we involuntarily become children once more. The soul sheds all that it has artificially acquired, to be what it was in its prime and probably will be again some day. Anyone who, like myself, has wandered among the wild mountains, has feasted his eyes on their fantastic shapes, and has eagerly inhaled the vivifying atmosphere of lofty passes—will readily understand why I long to reproduce these magical impressions.

When at length we reached the top of Gut-Gora, we stood a while to enjoy the view. A grey cloud still capped the mountain, and its cold breath conveyed a threat of approaching storm; but eastward all was so clear and golden that my companion and I were oblivious to the danger. Yes, even the captain forgot it. In simple-hearted persons such as he, a sense of the beauty and greatness of nature is stronger and a hundred times more real than in us enraptured writers who are accustomed to recording our thoughts upon paper.

'You, I take it, are familiar with this magnificent picture?' I asked him.

'Oh, yes, just as one can get used to the whistle of bullets, or at least hide one's alarm.'

'I have been told that there are veterans to whom that music is actually agreeable.'

'Of course it may be agreeable, but only because it makes the heart beat faster. Look,' he went on, pointing to the east, 'what a country!'

Hardly ever before, indeed, had I seen such a panorama. Beneath us lay the Koyshaursky Valley, intersected by the Aragva and the other river, like two silver threads. A bluish mist was gliding along, escaping from the warm rays of morning as it poured into the narrow pass nearby; to right and left were mountain ridges, towering tier upon tier, criss-crossing, long-drawn-out, covered with snowdrifts and patched with scrub. Far away were these mountains, but no two of the crags resembled one another; and all the snows flamed crimson with so gay a colour and looked so bright, that one would have liked to stay and watch for ever. The sun was just peeping from behind the dark-blue mountain, which only trained eyes could distinguish from the threatening storm-cloud; but this sun was backed by a blood-red band, to which my fellow-traveller drew my attention.

'I told you,' he exclaimed, 'that the weather would be bad. We must hurry up if we don't want to leave our bones on Mount Krestovoy.'

'Go ahead!' he shouted to the drivers.

Leading the horses by the bridle and using the brakes, they began the descent. On the right, the bank rose precipitously; on the left, there was so long and steep a declivity that an Ossete village at the bottom looked like a swallow's nest. I shuddered to think that often, perhaps every month, upon this road where there was not room for two carts to pass, an express messenger would tempt the perilous slope without troubling to get out of his rickety vehicle. One of our drivers was a Russian peasant from Yaroslavl, the other was an Ossete. The latter led the middle horse of the troika with the utmost care, but our easy-going Russian did not even trouble to get down from the box. When I told him he might do well to be a little more careful, were it only for the sake of my trunk, since I had certainly no wish to climb after it into that abyss, he answered:

'Yes, Master, God grant that we shan't end our journey there. We shouldn't be the first.'

He was right. We barely missed ending our journey that way; and if more people should think about the matter they would realize that when we keep alive it is rarely because we have taken pains to do so.

But perhaps you are impatient for the end of Bela's story? I must remind you that I am not writing a novelette, but notes of travel, so I cannot make the captain go on with his recital until he chooses to do so. Thus you will have to wait a while. Or, if you like, you can skip a few pages. Still, I advise you not to do that, for my account of how we got across the Krestovoy range (which highbrows like to call Mount Saint-Christopher) is really worth reading.

Well, from Gut-Gora we went down into the Chertovy Valley. 'The Valley of the Devil'—a name full of romance. As soon as you hear it, you picture the nest of the Evil Spirit amid inaccessible rocks. But you are making a mistake. 'Chertovy' does not come from 'chort', devil, but from 'cherta', boundary, for the river marks the

BELA

Georgian frontier. This valley was backed by snowdrifts, strongly reminding me of Saratov, Tambov, and other charming centres of Russian life.

'There is Krestovoy,' said the captain, as we went down into Chertovy Valley, pointing to a hill shrouded in snow. It was surmounted by a cross of black stone, past which led a barely discernible road. This was only used when the snows on the flank of the hill were in a dangerous state; but our drivers, declaring there was as yet no risk of an avalanche and wishing to spare the horses, circled the eminence instead of climbing it. While we were making this detour, we met five Ossetes. They offered us their services, and, gripping the wheels, shouting in unison, they began to help our carts along through the snow. Truly the way was perilous. On the right were poised above our heads huge masses of snow, looking ready to hurtle down into the valley at the first gust of wind. The narrow track was partly covered by snow, which in some places gave way beneath our feet, while in others it had been thawed by the sun's rays and had then frozen. On these ice-sheets we found it difficult to keep our footing, and the horses actually fell. On the left yawned a deep crevasse, in which there was a stream, now hidden beneath an icy crust, now foaming amid swarthy boulders. In two hours we had not yet skirted Mount Krestovoy—having advanced no more than a mile and a half.

Meanwhile the storm-clouds had lowered, we had been battered by hailstones, and it began to snow. The wind, blowing fiercely down the valley, was roaring and whistling like the very devil. The stone cross vanished amid the vapours which crowded upon us thick and fast from the east. As to that cross, by the way, it was, according to a widely credited tradition, erected by Peter the Great when making a royal progress through the Caucasus. In actual fact, Peter never came farther into the Caucasus than Daghestan. Besides, the cross itself tells us, by means of an inscription in large letters, that it was put up in 1824 by the orders of General Ermoloff. However, notwithstanding the inscription, the Peter legend has gained such general acceptance that it is hard to say which story we should believe—especially if your temperament inclines you to doubt the written word.

We had to make our way downhill for another three miles across rocks coated with ice in order to reach the posting-station at Kobi. The horses were tired out, we were chilled to the bone, the snow-storm got worse and worse, and could have given points and a beating to one of our northern blizzards, for its howling was fiercer, more sorrowful, more melancholy.

'Exile' (thus did I apostrophize myself), 'you are in the habit of lamenting your expulsion from the wide, free, and open steppes. There, you say, you could soar with cold but unfettered pinions, whereas here you bleat about being restricted and confined, and liken yourself to a prisoned eagle dashing its wings against the iron bars of its cage!'

'The storm's gaining on us,' said the captain. 'Look, you can see nothing but mist and snow. Before we know where we are, we shall roll over a precipice or get stuck in a ravine; and lower down, I suppose, we shall find the Baidara so much swollen that we shall never be able to cross. It's a fine place, Asia; the rivers no less than the people. You can't depend on any of them.'

The drivers thrashed the horses while volleying abuse. The poor beasts snorted, balked, wouldn't or couldn't budge, though the whips were reddened with blood from their lacerated flanks.

'Your Honour,' said one of the men at last, 'really we can't get to Kobi tonight. Hadn't we better turn off to the left while it's still possible? I can see black spots on the side of the mountain. Only Tartar huts, of course, but we shall be able to shelter from the storm. These fellows say they can get us there if you give them some vodka,' he added, pointing to the Ossetes.

'I know, Brother; I know without your telling me,' answered the captain. 'What beasts they are. Any excuse to get vodka!'

'Still,' I put in, 'you must know that without them we should be even worse off.'

'Agreed, agreed,' he muttered. 'Confound these guides, all the same. They scent out any chance of getting a little coin, and without them one can't find the way.'

So we turned to the left and, somehow or other, after a good deal of trouble, we reached our miserable refuge, consisting of two Tartar huts, built out of slabs of stone and large cobbles and surrounded by a wall. Our tatterdemalion hosts welcomed us with effusion. I learned afterwards that the government paid and fed them on condition that they gave accommodation to travellers overtaken by storm.

'It's just as well we've had to lie up,' I said, as I sat down near the fire. 'Now you'll be able to go on with the story of Bela. I was sure you hadn't finished it.'

BELA

'Why were you so sure of that?' he asked, with a sly smile.

'Because it's not in the nature of things that a story which began in so unusual a way should have an everyday sort of ending.'

'Well, you've guessed right.'

'I'm glad of that.'

'It's all very well for you to be glad, but my memories of the affair are sorrowful. She was a very fine girl, Bela. In the end I got to feel towards her as if she had been my own daughter, and she became very fond of me. I should tell you that I have no near relatives to think about. For twenty years I have heard no news of my father or my mother. As for taking a wife, I never dreamed of doing so in my younger days, and it would be foolish to think of such a thing now. Naturally, then, I was glad to make a pet of Bela. She used to sing songs to us, or dance a Caucasian dance—the lezghinka. A wonderful folk-dancer, she was. I have watched our fine young ladies in their ballroom dances at the provincial capital, and twenty years ago I was at a swagger ball in Moscow; but that sort of dancing was not in the same street with Bela's for beauty. Gregory Aleksandrovich decked her out like a doll, pampered and fondled her, and it was a marvel the way in which her beauty increased. The tan disappeared from her face and hands, so that in the end her cheeks were quite rosy. She was always cheerful, and I never wanted anything in the world except to make her laugh. God rest her soul.'

'What happened when she heard about her father's death?'

'We kept the news from her as long as we could—while she was getting used to her situation. When she was told of it, she wept for two days, but then she forgot.

'Things couldn't have gone on better than they did for four months. I have already told you that Gregory Aleksandrovich had a passion for going out shooting. Often he had simply itched to make for the woods in pursuit of boar or wild goat; but now he never went outside the ramparts. Then came a time when I noticed that he had begun to brood again; to pace up and down the room, arms crossed behind his back. At length, without having said a word to anyone, he departed on a shooting expedition, and was away for the whole morning. This happened again, and again, more and more frequently.

'"A bad business," I said to myself. "They must have fallen out."

'One morning when I went to his rooms I

saw—I can see it now in fancy—Bela sitting on the bed wearing a black silk overall. She was deathly pale, and looked so sorrowful that I was alarmed.

'"Where's Pechorin?" I asked.

'"Out shooting."

'"Did he go early today?"

'She made no reply, evidently finding it difficult to speak.

'"No, he left yesterday," she at length managed to explain, with a deep sigh.

'"You don't think anything's happened to him?"

'"Yesterday I thought and thought all day," she answered, weeping. "I pictured the various accidents that could have happened, fancying that a tusker might have gored him, or perhaps the Chechens have lassoed him in the mountains. But now it only seems to me that he doesn't love me any more."

'"Truly, my darling, you couldn't imagine anything worse than that."

'She wept even more pitifully, but then proudly raised her head, dried her tears, and went on:

'"If he doesn't love me any more, what prevents his sending me home? I shouldn't offer any objection. Indeed, if matters go on like this,

BELA

I shall go without waiting to be sent. I am not his slave. I am a chieftain's daughter."

'I began to argue with her.

'"Listen, Bela," I said. "You really can't expect him to stay here all the time, as if he were tied to your apron-strings. He's a young fellow to whom the wish for hunting wild creatures is second nature. Besides he needs air and exercise. But if you have fits of the sulks on that account, you'll soon begin to bore him."

'"True, quite true," she exclaimed. "I will be cheerful."

'With an outburst of laughter, she seized her tambourine, began to sing, to dance, and to gambol round me. But this did not last. Once more she flung herself on the bed and covered her face with her hands.

'What on earth was I to do with her? I had never had much truck with women. I thought and thought, wondering how to console her, but nothing occurred to me, and for a good while neither of us said a word. It was a very trying state of affairs.

'At length I said to her: "If you like, we'll go for a stroll on the ramparts. The weather is lovely." This was in September. Actually, the day was glorious; sunshine and not too hot. The circle of mountains surrounded us like a huge saucer. We went out, and walked to and fro on the ramparts without speaking. At length she sat down on the turf, and I sat beside her. Indeed as I look back, it seems a little ridiculous, for I was shepherding her as a nursemaid shepherds a child.

'The fortress stood upon an elevation, and the view from the ramparts was splendid. On one side was a wide stretch of meadowland, intersected by a few gullies, and ending in a forest which stretched up to the sierras; here and there one could see the smoke from villages, and droves of horses in between. On the other side ran a gleaming river, whose banks were lined by dense scrub, covering the flinty mounds which were spurs of the central chain of the Caucasus. Sitting as we were in the salient of a bastion, we got a good outlook in both directions. Then I caught sight of a man mounted on a grey horse who came out of the forest, rode nearer and nearer, and at length, having reached the bank of the stream about three hundred yards away, began to make his steed whirl round and round like mad. A most unexpected sight.

'"Look, Bela," I said. "Your eyes are younger than mine. What's that fellow up to? Is he doing it to amuse himself, do you suppose?"

'She looked where I pointed, and cried: "Why, it's Kazbich."

'"That ruffian? Has he posted himself down there to make fun of us by showing off his tricks of horsemanship?"

'Looking again, I saw that it really was Kazbich, with his face deeply bronzed and his clothing ragged and filthy as usual.

'"That's my father's horse," said Bela, seizing my hand. She trembled like an aspen leaf, and her eyes blazed.

'"Aha, my dear," I thought, "in you, likewise the blood of robber chieftains has a word to say."

'"Come here," I called to the sentry. "Take good aim and try to shoot that chap out of his saddle. If you manage it, I'll give you a silver rouble."

'"Very good, Your Honour; but the beggar won't keep still."

'"Tell him he must," I said banteringly.

'"Look out, my fine fellow," shouted the sentry, waving his hand, "but do stop spinning like a top."

'Kazbich did, in fact, stop rotating, in order to hear what the sentry was calling. He must really have imagined that a parley had begun. My grenadier took aim. Bang! No good. It was a miss. As the smoke cleared, Kazbich spurred his mount, which sprang to the side. Rising in the stirrups, he shouted something in his own tongue, made a threatening movement with his whip—and galloped away.

'"Aren't you ashamed of yourself?" I asked the sentry.

'"Your Honour, I made sure I should get him. But you know what devils these Tartars are. Very hard to kill."

'A quarter of an hour later Pechorin came back from his shooting expedition. Bela flung her arms round his neck, uttering not a word of complaint nor reproaching him in any way for his prolonged absence. I myself felt angry with him.

'"Look here," I said. "Just now Kazbich turned up beside the river, and we took a pot-shot at him. He may try that game with you soon. These mountaineers are vengeful. Do you suppose he never guessed that you had a hand in the Azamat affair? I wouldn't mind betting that he recognized Bela on the ramparts. I know that a year ago he was passionately in love with her. He told me so. If he hoped to get money together and buy himself a wife in the Tartar fashion, you may take it that Bela was the woman he wanted."

BELA

'Pechorin thought the matter over, and then answered:

'"Certainly I shall have to watch out. Bela, from now on you mustn't show yourself on the ramparts."

'That evening I discussed matters with him at considerable length. I was vexed that he had shown any change in his feelings towards the poor girl. In addition to leaving her by herself while he went out shooting for half the day, his manner to her had become cold, he rarely caressed her, and she was obviously losing flesh, her dear little face looked pinched, and her big eyes were less bright than they had been.

'I often said to her: "Bela, what are you sighing about? Are you unhappy?"—"No."—"Is there anything you particularly want?"—"No." —"Are you pining for your kinsfolk?"—"I have no kinsfolk."—Sometimes except for "yes" and "no" I could not get a word out of her.

'I talked things over once more with Pechorin, and this is what he said.

'"Maksim Maksimich, I have a difficult character. Whether it is the result of my nurture, or of the way in which God thought fit to create me, I can't tell you. All I know is that if I bring unhappiness to others, I am myself no less unhappy. Not much consolation of course; but that's how matters are. In my early youth, as soon as I left home and was no longer looked after by my relatives, I began to indulge in a mad round of the pleasures which money can command, and, I need hardly tell you, that I speedily had a surfeit of them. Then I plunged into the life of the fashionable world, and soon that, too, sickened me. I fell in love with society beauties, and my affection was returned; but at bottom these affairs merely tickled my imagination and ministered to my vanity, while my heart remained untouched. I began to read, to study; but the sciences likewise bored me. It became plain to me that neither fame nor happiness depend in any way on a mastery of the sciences: for really happy people are apt to be nit-wits; as for fame, it comes to the successful, and to be successful you need merely have a keen eye for the main chance. These reflections were extremely discouraging.—Soon the authorities sent me to the Caucasus, where I have spent the happiest time in my life. My hope was that the bullets of the Chechens would not bore me, but alas within a few months I grew so accustomed to the sound of them and to the imminence of death, that the buzzing of a gnat seemed more important. The upshot was that I became more bored than ever, having lost what was practically my last hope.

"'When I saw Bela in my own rooms here, when for the first time, having taken her on my knees, I kissed her raven tresses, I (being an idiot) believed her to be an angel sent to me by a merciful providence. Once more I was mistaken. The love of a savage woman is no better than the love of a fine lady. The ignorance and simplicity of the one are no less wearisome than is the coquetry of the other. If you like, I don't mind admitting that I still love her; that I am grateful to her for some minutes of intense happiness; that I would give my life for her; but the long and the short of it is that she bores me. I don't know whether to regard myself as fool or knave; but this is certain, at any rate, that I am very much to be pitied—perhaps more than she is. My mind has been corrupted by the world, my fancy is fickle, my heart insatiable, everything seems petty; I get used to sorrow as quickly as to enjoyment, and my life grows emptier day by day. One expedient is still left me—travel. As soon as possible, I shall start. Not for Europe (God preserve me from it), but for America, Arabia, India, and perhaps I shall have the luck to die on the way. At least I am sure that this last consolation will not be too

BELA

speedily exhausted—with the help of storms and bad roads."

'He went on talking in that strain for a long time, and his words have been graven into my memory, for never before or since have I heard such things from a young fellow of twenty-five —and, please God, I shall never hear them again. What a strange thing. Tell me, please,' went on the captain, turning towards me, 'you, I understand, were in the capital not very long ago. Can it be that all the young fellows there are of the same sort as Pechorin?'

I answered that he would find a great many to voice similar sentiments, and that some of them would actually believe what they said; but that disillusionment, like other fashions that begin in the highest circles, had seeped down to the lowest, where it had worn threadbare. The result was that of late those who most of all and most genuinely were bored were now inclined to hide their unhappiness as a vice.

The captain, who could not understand these niceties, shook his head and replied with a shrewd smile:

'I suppose the French made boredom fashionable?'

'No, it was the English.'

'Ah, that explains things, for the English have always been heavy drinkers.'

This reminded me of a man I had known in Moscow, who assured me that Byron was nothing more than a drunkard. Besides, the captain's remark was comprehensible enough. Having determined to be an abstainer, he naturally tried to persuade himself that all the misfortune in the world came from drink.

Kazbich did not turn up again at the fort. Still, I don't know why, I could not get rid of the idea that his appearance beside the river had had a meaning in it, and that he must be plotting mischief.

'There came a time when Pechorin wanted me to come out with him after boar. For a long time I refused, saying that wild pigs were nothing new to me. Still in the end he succeeded in inducing me to agree. Accompanied by five soldiers, we set out early in the morning. Till ten o'clock we drew the coverts and beat the beds of rushes—not a sign of game.

'"Hadn't we better give up the boar and go home?" I asked.

'He wanted to stick it, however. Evidently this was not one of our lucky days. But Gregory Aleksandrovich, though we were hot and tired, would not desist until we had got what we came out for. That's the sort of fellow he was, a man who always says "Let's get on with it," and had certainly been a spoiled child, "mother's pet". At length, towards noon, we roused an accursed boar. Bang! Bang! But we both missed, and the beast vanished among the reeds. A bad day for sportsmen. So, having rested a little, we started on our homeward way.

'We rode side by side, silently, our pace involuntarily slackening; but we had nearly reached the fortress, which was still hidden from us by the brushwood, when unexpectedly we heard gunshots ahead of us. We stared at one another, both struck by the same suspicion; then galloped helter-skelter in the direction of the shooting, and looked. On the ramparts the soldiers were massed together, pointing at the plain, where a horseman who held something in front of him on the saddle was riding away at top speed. Gregory Aleksandrovich yelled, for all the world like a Chechen, unslung his rifle, and pursued—I with him.

'Fortunately, because we had had an unsuccessful day, our horses were not tired out. They galloped with a will, and from moment to moment we drew nearer to the chase. Soon I recognized Kazbich, but I could not see clearly what he was holding in front of him. How-

BELA

ever, getting abreast of Pechorin, I shouted to him:

'"That's Kazbich."

'He looked at me, nodded, and lashed his horse.

'At length we were within range. The bandit's steed was exhausted, or at any rate had less go than ours, and despite his utmost efforts the ruffian could not gain on us. I think that, at this instant, he must have longed for Karagyoz.

'Then I saw that Pechorin was taking aim while he rode at full gallop.

'"Don't fire," I called to him. "Save your ammunition. We shall overtake him."

'Youth, youth, so apt to lose its head at a critical moment.

'A shot rang out, for he did not heed my warning. The bullet struck one of the hind legs of Kazbich's mount, which staggered on for another ten paces, stumbled, and fell on its knees. Kazbich jumped off, and then we could see what he had been holding in front of him, a woman muffled in a veil, Bela. Yes, poor Bela. He shouted something to me in his own language, and brandished his dagger over her. There was no time to loose. I took my turn at shooting, and successfully. My bullet hit him in the shoulder, for his arm dropped. When the smoke cleared, we could see the wounded horse stretched on the ground, and Bela lying close by. Kazbich, having thrown away his carbine, was making for the cover of the brushwood, clambering up the rocks like a cat. I wanted to pick him off with another shot, but I couldn't reload in time. We dismounted and ran to Bela. Poor girl, she had fainted, but the blood was still gushing in torrents from her wound.

'Black-hearted villain. If he was ruthless enough to strike, why couldn't he have finished her off with a gash in the heart, but he had given her a robber's stab in the back. She was mercifully unconscious. We tore her veil into strips and bound up her wound as best we could. Pechorin unavailingly kissed her cold lips. Nothing could bring her to.

'The ensign mounted. I lifted Bela from the ground and somehow or other managed to place her on the saddle in front of him. He clasped her in his arms, and we rode slowly towards the fort. After a few minutes silence, Gregory Aleksandrovich said to me:

'"Look here, Maksim Maksimich, we shall never get her home alive at this pace."

'"You're right," I answered; so we took the choice of evils and spurred our horses into a canter.

'A crowd was waiting for us at the gates. As carefully as possible we carried the stricken girl to Pechorin's quarters, and sent for the regimental surgeon. He was damnably drunk. Nevertheless, he came, examined the wound, and announced that she could not live more than twenty-four hours—but he was mistaken.'

'Did she get well, then?' I asked the captain.

'No, but the surgeon was wrong, for she lived two days.'

'Please explain to me how Kazbich had managed to get hold of her.'

'It was like this. In spite of Pechorin's orders, she went out of the fortress and down to the river. Since it was very hot, she sat on a rock and dabbled her feet in the water. Then Kazbich crept up from behind, pounced on her, tied up her mouth, dragged her into the bushes where he had left his horse, mounted and rode off with his prey. She managed to free her mouth and scream. The sentries aimed and fired, but missed. Then we turned up, and gave chase, as I have told you.'

'Why did Kazbich want to kidnap her?'

'Why? Everyone knows the Circassians are a thievish crowd. They simply can't resist carrying off whatever isn't nailed down. Even useless things will be stolen. You can hardly blame them for what is second nature to them. Besides, he had wanted her for a long time.'

'So Bela died of her wound?'

'Yes, she died, after many hours of suffering—which were painful and exhausting to us onlookers as well. At about ten in the evening she recovered consciousness. We were sitting beside the bed when she opened her eyes and began to call for Pechorin.

'"I am here, close to you, my darling," he said, fondling her hand.

'"I'm dying," she moaned.

'We tried to reassure her, declaring that the surgeon was absolutely convinced she would get well. She shook her head and turned her face to the wall. She did not want to die. . . .

'In the night she was delirious. Her head was burning hot, and from time to time her whole body was shaken by shivering fits. She rambled on about her father and her brother; wanted to go to the mountains, to go home. Also she talked about Pechorin, gave him various affectionate names, or reproached him for having ceased to love her.

'He listened without a word, resting his face on his hands; but, as far as I could see, he did not shed any tears. Indeed he may have been unable to weep, or may have controlled the desire. I can't tell. For my part, I never saw anything so lamentable.

'In the morning the delirium was over. For an hour she lay motionless, poor dear, so weak that one could hardly be sure she was breathing. Then she got a little better, and started talking, but you would never guess what it was about. Such a thought would have come to her only on her deathbed. She began to lament that she was not a Christian, that in the other world her soul would therefore never meet the soul of Gregory Aleksandrovich, and that some other woman would be his mate in paradise. It occurred to me that we could baptise her before she died. I suggested this to her. She looked at me dubiously, and for a long time could not utter a word. Then she said that she would die in the faith of her fathers.

'Thus the day passed. She changed terribly in the course of that day. The pallid cheeks became more sunken, her eyes looked larger and larger, her lips were burning. She said she felt as hot inside as if her chest had been filled with red-hot iron.

'Another night came. We had not closed our eyes, nor moved from the bedside. She was suffering horribly; she groaned; and only from time to time when the pain abated a little did she try to persuade Gregory Aleksandrovich that she was better, beg him to go and lie down, and kiss his hand of which she kept fast hold. Towards morning, feeling that death was near, she tossed about, dislodging the bandage, and the bleeding began again. When we had rebandaged the wound, she was quieter for a little while, and asked Pechorin to kiss her. He dropped on his knees close to the bed, raised her head from the pillows, and pressed his lips on her cheeks which were now growing cold; she clasped his neck with her trembling fingers, as if in that kiss she might hope to pass on her soul to him. Indeed she did well to die, for how could she have borne it if Gregory Aleksandrovich had forsaken her? Yet I am sure he would have done so, sooner or later.

'For half of the next day she was less restless, being silent and submissive when our surgeon tormented her with his fomentations and his mixtures.

'"Good God, man," I said to him, "you yourself told us that the case was hopeless; why then do you go on bothering her with what you know can do no good?"

'"After all, Maksim Maksimich," he replied, "surely it's better that we should have easy consciences?"

'An easy conscience!

'A little past noon she began to suffer from thirst. We opened the window, but it was even hotter in the yard than in the room; we put lumps of ice round the bed; but nothing helped. I knew that this intolerable thirst was a sign of the coming of the end, and I said as much to Pechorin.

'"Water, water," she kept on calling in a hoarse voice, as she tossed and writhed.

'Gregory Aleksandrovich, who was as white as a sheet, took a glass, filled it with water, and brought it to her.

'Covering my eyes with my hands, I began to murmur a prayer—I forget which one. My dear fellow, I have seen many men die, in hospital and on the field of battle; but I never saw anything like this. I must admit that what grieved me most is that when she was dying, she never gave me a thought, though I loved her like a father. May God forgive me. I tell you frankly, that's the way I'm made; I wanted her to think of me when she was dying. . . .

'She had hardly drunk the water than she felt easier, but within two or three minutes all was over. We put a mirror to her lips, and the surface was not dimmed. I led Pechorin out of the room, and we went on to the ramparts, where we walked up and down for a long time without a word, our arms folded behind. His face showed nothing out of the common, but I felt sorrowful; so sorrowful that I could have died of grief then and there. At length he sat on the ground, in the shade, and began to trace figures in the sand with his forefinger. I, for form's sake chiefly, wanted to console him, so I began to talk; but he raised his head and burst out laughing. His laughter gave me the creeps; and I went away to order the coffin.

'I will own that it was partly a longing for distraction which led me to occupy myself about this matter. I had a piece of Persian silk, and I lined the coffin with it, while for outward adornment I used some silver braid which Gregory Aleksandrovich had bought for Bela.

'Next day, early in the morning, we buried her outside the fortress, close to the river, and only a few steps from the place where she had last sat. Acacias and elders grow round her grave. I should have liked to put up a cross, but that would have been unsuitable, for, you see, she wasn't a Christian.'

'What became of Pechorin?' I asked.

'For a good while he was out of sorts, got very thin, poor fellow. But thenceforward we never said a word to one another about Bela. I saw he would find that disagreeable, and what would have been the use? Three months after her death, he was transferred to another regiment, and went to Georgia. I have never met him since.—Oh, but I remember someone told me not long ago that he had gone back to Russia, I don't know to what corps. To us here news comes slowly.'

Then he broke into a long dissertation about the inconvenience of getting news a year late. The captain was only talking, now, to stifle the sad memories he had evoked.

I did not interrupt him, and in fact I hardly listened.

In about an hour we were able to make a fresh start. The snowstorm was over, the sky had cleared, and we set out. On the road I led the conversation back to the story of Bela and Pechorin.

'Did you ever hear what became of Kazbich?' I asked.

'Kazbich? I don't know. I have been told that among the half-savage Shapsughs there is a man of that name, a dare-devil who, wearing a red tunic, rides across the steppe at a walking pace under fire, and salutes politely when bullets whiz past his ears. But I doubt if that's our man.'

BELA

At Kobi I bade farewell to Maksim Maksimich. I was going to use post-horses, and he, owing to the heavy nature of his baggage, could not keep up with me. We never expected to meet again, but we did, and if you like I will let you know about it. You will agree, I think, that he is a man worthy of respect? If you admit that much, I shall be fully rewarded for telling you what has, perhaps, been rather too long a yarn.

MAKSIM MAKSIMICH

MAKSIM MAKSIMICH

When I had parted from Maksim Maksimich, I went as quickly as I could through the Terek and Daryal valleys. I ate my midday meal at Kazbek, had tea at Lars, and hurried on to Vladikavkaz for supper. No need to bother you with a description of the mountains and the views, in words which would convey little, especially to persons who have never seen them. Least of all shall I burden my pages with statistics, which I am quite sure no one would read.

I stayed at the hotel where all travellers put up—a place where no one can roast a pheasant or make soup, for the three broken-down fellows whose job it is to attend to such matters are so stupid and so much given to drink as to be absolutely undependable.

I was told that this place must be my quarters for three days, since the convoy from Ekaterinograd had not yet come, and therefore was not ready to return. In this part of the world a convoy is called an 'occasion'. It was a very tiresome occasion indeed, but a bad pun is no consolation to a Russian, so I thought that the best way of passing the time would be to write down

MAKSIM MAKSIMICH

Maksim Maksimich's story of Bela, and I did so without any idea that it would be the first of a series of tales. A trifling circumstance may sometimes have remarkable results. You probably don't know that these convoys, these 'occasions', consist of half a company of infantry with a field-gun or two to protect the carts that pass through Kabardia on the road between Vladikavkaz and Ekaterinograd.

The first day I was bored stiff, but early next morning a carriage drew up at the door of the hotel. In it was Maksim Maksimich. We met as old friends. I offered him a share of my room. He was not slow to accept, slapping me on the shoulder and actually screwing up his mouth into a smile of a sort. A queer customer, he was.

Maksim Maksimich had an intimate knowledge of the culinary art. He roasted a pheasant admirably, pouring over it some brine in which cucumbers had been pickled; and I was certain that had he not been there I should have had to eat it dry, without any sauce. A bottle of good wine made in the district helped us to forget that there was only one course. When we had finished our meal, we lighted our pipes. As we smoked, I sat close by the window, but he preferred the neighbourhood of the stove for the day was raw and cold.

MAKSIM MAKSIMICH

We were silent, having nothing to talk about. He had already told me what was interesting about his own experiences, and I had no more to say to him concerning myself. Looking quietly out of the window I contemplated the numerous little houses scattered along the banks of the Terek, a river which broadens here as it winds among the trees. Farther on came a glimpse of blue, lofty mountains among which Kazbek was conspicuous in its cardinal's hat (white instead of red). I was moodily bidding the range farewell, being sorry to leave it.

Thus we sat for a long time. The sun was not far from the cold peaks, and a pale mist was beginning to rise from the valleys, when I heard in the road the bells of a troika and the shouts of drivers. Some wagons containing dirty Armenians drove into the yard, followed by an empty travelling-calash, whose easy running, good make, and smart aspect gave it a foreign stamp. Behind it walked a man heavily moustached, wearing livery, but rather too well dressed for an ordinary footman. Even so, one could not doubt his occupation when one saw the swagger way in which he knocked the ashes out of his pipe and heard the tone in which he called to the coachman. He must be the spoiled servant of an easy-going master—must be a sort of Russian Figaro, in fact.

'Tell me, my man,' I called through the window, 'what's that? The convoy, isn't it, which has just come?'

He looked at me impertinently, adjusted his necktie, and turned away. An Armenian who was close to him smiled and, answering for him, said it really was the convoy, and would be returning tomorrow.

'Thank goodness,' put in Maksim Maksimich, coming up to the window at this moment. 'What a wonderfully fine calash,' he added. 'It must belong to an official who is going to hold an enquiry at Tiflis. Obviously he doesn't know what sort of roads we have here. I'm not joking. They'll knock even an English carriage to flinders. I should like to know who the owner is. Let's go and find out.'

We went into the passage. At the other end the door was ajar, and we could see into the room. The footman and the coachman were dragging some trunks across the floor.

'Hullo, my man,' said the staff-captain, 'tell me, whose is that fine calash? It's a wonderful carriage.'

The footman did not turn round, but muttered something to himself as he opened one of the

MAKSIM MAKSIMICH

boxes. Maksim Maksimich, losing his temper, tapped the ill-mannered fellow on the shoulder, saying: 'I asked you a question.'

'Whose calash is it? My master's, of course.'

'Well, what's your master's name?'

'Pechorin.'

'Pechorin, you say? Good Lord! Was he ever stationed in the Caucasus before?' exclaimed Maksim Maksimich, twitching one of my sleeves, his eyes sparkling with delight.

'I think so, Sir; but I haven't been with him long.'

'I know him, then, if he's called Gregory Aleksandrovich. Your master and I were chums for a long time,' said Maksim Maksimich giving the footman another push on the shoulder, a friendly one this time, but violent enough to make the man stagger.

'Excuse me, Sir,' said the servant, 'but you're really hindering my work.' He frowned.

'Don't worry about that, man. I tell you your master and I were chums. We lived together. Why isn't he here? Where did he stay?'

The footman answered that Pechorin had left the carriage to have supper with Colonel N., and would probably spend the night in that gentleman's quarters.

'So he won't be here this evening? Hasn't he

MAKSIM MAKSIMICH

told you to go back with some of his things? If so, explain to him that Maksim Maksimich is here. No more. He'll know who I am. I'll tip you eighty copecks for your trouble.'

The footman made a wry face, for the gratuity was not a handsome one. Still, he said he would give the message.

'Pechorin will soon be here,' declared the captain exultantly. 'I'll go outside and wait there till he comes. Sorry I don't know Colonel N.'

Maksim Maksimich sat on a stool outside the gate, while I went to my room. I admit that I awaited the coming of this man Pechorin with considerable impatience. Though the staff-captain's story about Bela and the ensign had not given me a very favourable impression of the latter, certain traits in his character had aroused my interest.

In an hour one of the inefficient servants turned up with a steaming samovar and a tea-pot. Going to the window I called out: 'Maksim Maksimich, would you like a glass of tea?'

'No thank you,' he said. 'I don't feel inclined for it.'

'You'd better drink some. It's getting late, and it's rather cold.'

'No thanks. I'd rather not.'

'Just as you please.'

MAKSIM MAKSIMICH

I began to drink some by myself. Then in ten minutes he came in, saying:

'Oh well, praps you're right. I'll have some tea after all. It's such a long wait. That footman must have got to him a good while ago. Something's keeping him.'

He drank his tea quickly, refused a second glass, and went out again, being obviously restless. He seemed annoyed because Pechorin had ignored his message—all the more because he had recently, in the Bela story, laid so much stress upon their friendship, and because an hour ago he had been confident that Pechorin would hurry along the instant the old companion's name was mentioned.

It was late and darkness had fallen when I opened the window once more and called to Maksim Maksimich that it was time to come to bed. He answered with an unintelligible growl. I tried again, but this time there was no reply.

Wrapping myself in a cloak, I lay down on the heated couch, leaving a candle alight on the other end of it. Soon I was dozing, and should have been sound asleep had not Maksim Maksimich awakened me by coming into the room after a considerable time. He flung his pipe on to the table, stamped to and fro, raked the stove,

MAKSIM MAKSIMICH

and at length settled down; but he went on coughing, clearing his throat, and fidgeting.

'Are the bugs worrying you?' I asked.

'Yes, bugs, curse them,' he answered, sighing.

Next morning I woke early, but Maksim Maksimich was before me. He had vanished. I found him sitting on his stool outside the gates.

'I must go and see the commandant,' he said. 'If Pechorin arrives, please send for me.'

'Of course,' I replied.

He hurried off, as if his limbs had once more been animated with the strength and suppleness of youth.

That morning was fresh and lovely. Golden clouds were gathering above the mountains, and looked like another range behind the first. In front of the gates was a big square. The market being held there was crowded, for it was Sunday. Barefooted Ossete boys carrying on their shoulders baskets filled with honeycomb, pestered me to buy, but I swore at them, finding them a nuisance, for I had been infected by the staff-captain's uneasiness.

In less than ten minutes, I caught sight of the man for whom we were waiting. He came into the square on the farther side, accompanied by Colonel N., who, having walked with him up to the entrance of the hotel, said goodbye and made for the fort. I instantly sent one of the servants for Maksim Maksimich.

Pechorin's footman went out to meet his master and told him that the horses were just being harnessed. Handing over a cigar-case, the man received instructions and hurried off. Pechorin, having lighted up, yawned two or three times and sat down on a bench outside the gate. Now let me give you a description of him.

He was of middle height and graceful build, having a slim waist but broad shoulders suggesting a vigorous constitution, which would be steeled against the hardships of a wandering life that involved frequent changes of climate, and would make him equally immune to the enervating effects of libertinage in the capital and the emotional storms of youth. His velveteen coat was dusty with travel, and was fastened only by the two lower buttons, so that it allowed glimpses of the spotless underlinen appropriate to a gentleman of fashion. His gloves, though soiled, were a perfect fit on his small aristocratic hands, and when he took them off I was struck by the slenderness of his fingers. His gait was easy and unhurried, and I noticed that he did not swing his arms as he walked—a sure sign of a reserved disposition.

Of course these are personal impressions based upon my own observation, and I don't expect the reader to swallow them whole with his eyes shut.

When he sat down on the bench his straight body seemed to double up as if there had been no bones in his spine. The position he assumed indicated nervous exhaustion, for he collapsed as Balzac's coquette (the heroine of *La Femme de Trente Ans*) collapsed into a deep armchair after the fatigues of a night in the ballroom. When I caught my first glimpse of his face I took him for no more than twenty-three, but later I should have given him a full thirty. His smile was quite youthful, and his skin was as soft as a woman's. Fair hair, curling by nature, formed a picturesque frame for his white, well-shaped forehead which on close observation was seen to be furrowed by a crisscross of fine lines, deepened no doubt when he grew angry or was otherwise strongly moved. Though the hair of his head was blonde, his moustache and eyebrows were black. In a man this signifies 'blue blood', just as a black mane and a black tail signify pedigree in a white horse.

I should add that his nose was rather short, that his teeth were dazzlingly white, and that he had hazel eyes; but about these eyes I must write a little more.

In the first place when he laughed, the eyes did not participate. Has the reader ever noticed this characteristic in anyone, and how it either indicates a bad temper, or else betrays profound and lasting melancholy? Again, through his half-lowered lashes, the eyes gleamed with what I can only call phosphorescence. This was not the outward manifestation of an inward spiritual fire, nor yet of vivid imagination, but a lustre like that of polished steel, cold though dazzling. His glance, brief but emphatic and piercing, gave the impression of an indiscreet question, and might even have been considered rude had it not been so nonchalant and tranquil.

Possibly all these opinions, which I have recorded as observations, really flashed into my mind because I knew certain details of his life, and another glimpse of him might have produced very different impressions. But since it is only from me that you are likely to hear about him, you will have to be satisfied with my account. Let me add, in conclusion, that he was exceedingly good-looking, and had one of those original faces which are apt to prove most attractive to women.

MAKSIM MAKSIMICH

The horses had been harnessed, and the bells of the troika sounded from time to time as the animals moved restlessly. Twice the footman had told his master that everything was ready for the start—but there was no sign of Maksim Maksimich. Luckily Pechorin was plunged in thought, with his eyes fixed on the ridge of the Caucasus, and he seemed in no hurry to be off. I went up to him, saying:

'If you can wait a little while, you'll have the pleasure of seeing an old friend.'

'Oh, yes,' he answered brusquely. 'They told me yesterday. But what's become of him?'

Turning towards the square, I saw Maksim Maksimich running towards us as fast as he could. In a minute or two he reached us, out of breath, and with sweat streaming down his face. Damp grey curls which had protruded from beneath his cap were sticking to his forehead. His knees were trembling. When he was on the point of flinging his arms round Pechorin's neck, the latter offered a hand rather coldly, though smiling civilly enough. The staff-captain was taken aback for a moment; then he seized the other's hand in both of his, but he still could not say a word.

'I'm so glad to see you, my dear Maksim Maksimich,' put in Pechorin. 'How are you?'

MAKSIM MAKSIMICH

'How are you? That's what I want to know,' replied the captain, stammeringly, and with tears in his eyes. 'It's years since we met. But where are you off to, now?'

'I'm going to Persia, and farther than that.'

'But not this very minute, surely? Won't the start keep for a little while, my dear fellow? We needn't part so soon when we haven't met for a long time.'

'Long or short, it's time for me to go, Maksim Maksimich,' was the answer.

'Good God, why are you in a hurry? There's such a lot I want to talk to you about, and I have so many things to ask you. Have you retired from the army? Is that so? Well, what have you been doing with yourself?'

'Bored to death, as usual,' replied Pechorin with a smile.

'Do you remember our life in the fortress? Fine shooting country, and you used to be so fond of shooting. Have you forgotten Bela?'

Turning rather pale, Pechorin answered:

'No, I remember Bela.'

Then he forced a yawn—or it seemed forced.

Maksim Maksimich begged him to put off the start for a couple of hours.

'We'll have a glorious dinner,' he said. 'I've a brace of pheasants, and the local wine is excellent. Not as good as you get in Georgia, but really worth drinking. We'll have a talk then. I want you to tell me about your life in St. Petersburg.'

'But really I've nothing to tell you, my dear Maksim Maksimich. It's goodbye, that's all. I've got to start now, for time presses. Thank you for not forgetting me.'

The captain knitted his brows. He was hurt and angry, but tried to hide these emotions.

'Forget you?' he muttered. 'No, I've forgotten nothing. Well, God be with you. I never thought it would be like this if we should meet again.'

'Oh well, oh well,' said Pechorin, putting a friendly hand on the other's shoulder. 'I haven't really changed, you know. But what can one do? Each of us has to walk along his own road. Perhaps we shall have another meeting. God alone knows.'

With that, he got into the calash, and the coachman lifted the reins.

'Stop! Stop!' said the staff-captain, gripping the carriage-door. 'There's something I've quite forgotten to ask. I still have a lot of your papers, Gregory Aleksandrovich. I've been lugging them about with me everywhere. Thought I might meet you in Georgia, but after all we've met here at last. What am I to do with them?'

'Whatever you please,' answered Pechorin. 'Now I must be off.'

'You're really going to Persia? When do you expect to be back?'

This the staff-captain shouted after the calash, which had already started. Pechorin waved his hand in a way which might be interpreted as expressing:

'Never, perhaps. What is there to come back for anyhow?'

We had long ceased to hear the bells of the troika, or the gride of wheels on the flinty road, but my poor old friend continued to stand where he was, deep in thought.

'Yes,' he said at last, with assumed indifference, though tears of vexation were brimming over from his eyes and coursing down his cheeks, 'of course we were close friends long ago. But what does he care about me now? I'm neither a rich man nor a high official, and I'm much older than he is. Did you notice what a dandified rig-out he was wearing? He might still have been in St. Petersburg. A smart calash, too. Such a lot of luggage, and a footman with damnable side!' Maksim Maksimich paused with a sarcastic smile. Then he went on: 'Tell me what you think of him. What the devil is taking him to Persia? It's ridiculous, simply ridiculous. I always knew he was undependable, a man one couldn't rely on. It's a pity, but I'm sure he'll come to a bad end. That's what's bound to happen. I've often said that no one thrives by forgetting old friends.'

He turned away to hide his agitation, and walked about the yard round his carriage, as if he were inspecting the wheels, but really his eyes were streaming with tears.

'Maksim Maksimich,' I said, going up to him, 'tell me, what are those papers Pechorin left in your care?'

'God may know, but I don't. Some sort of diary or memoirs, I believe.'

'What are you going to do with them?'

'Damned if I know. Make them into wads for cartridges, I suppose.'

'Better give them to me.'

He looked at me wonderingly, muttered something unintelligible while keeping his teeth clenched, and began to rummage one of the trunks in his carriage. He extracted a manuscript book, and flung it contemptuously on the ground. This was followed by a second, a third, a fourth, and more, until ten were lying there. It was both laughable and pitiable to watch him.

MAKSIM MAKSIMICH

'That's the lot,' he said. 'Let me congratulate you on your windfall.'

'Can I do with them whatever I want?'

'Have them printed in the papers, if you like. What's it matter to me? As you see, he doesn't treat me as a friend, and I'm certainly not a relative. True, I lived under the same roof with him for quite a while. So have I with a great many others.'

I picked up the manuscript books, and promptly carried them off, being afraid lest the donor might change his mind. Soon I was informed that the convoy was to start in an hour, and I gave orders that my carriage should be got ready. The staff-captain came into my room when I was putting on my cap. He, it seemed, was not ready for departure. He looked perplexed and chilled.

'Aren't you coming, Maksim Maksimich?' I asked.

'No.'

'Why not?'

'I haven't seen the commandant yet, and I have to hand over some munitions.'

'But I thought you'd already been to see him?'

'Of course I went this morning,' he said hesitatingly. 'But he was out, and I didn't wait.'

I understood. For the first time in his life

(perhaps) the poor fellow had let private affairs take precedence of his duty to the service. I had seen what he had gained thereby!

'I am very, very sorry, Maksim Maksimich,' I said, 'that we must part so soon.'

'How can we, old ignoramuses that we are, expect to keep pace with you vigorous youngsters? When Circassian bullets are flying about, you have a use for our company. But when we meet afterwards, you are hardly willing to shake hands.'

'I have done nothing to merit such reproaches, Maksim Maksimich.'

'Of course you haven't. I was speaking in general terms. I wish you luck, and a pleasant journey.'

Thus we parted, rather coldly. Good Maksim Maksimich had suddenly become a stubborn, crusty staff-captain. And why, if you please? Simply because Pechorin, from absence of mind or some other cause, had merely offered a hand to a man who wanted to embrace him. It is a sad spectacle when a youth loses his hopes and dreams, because the rosy veil through which he has hitherto contemplated the doings and feelings of his fellows has been ruthlessly torn away. True, he may be able to replace the old fancies by new ones, which will be no less transitory, but will nevertheless be sweet while they last. But Maksim Maksimich was too old for such new fancies. For as age advances the heart must harden and the mind narrow.

I departed alone.

PECHORIN'S DIARY

PREFACE

A LITTLE while ago I heard that Pechorin had died on his way back from Persia. This news was agreeable rather than otherwise, for it entitled me to publish the diary. I have seized the chance of putting my name to another man's work. I hope my readers will forgive the innocent fraud.

Now it behoves me to furbish up some sort of excuse for thus making public the secrets of a man whom I never knew. I should have been readily pardonable had I been his friend, for all can understand the deliberate indiscretion of a true friend. But I saw him no more than once, so I cannot feel for him that unaccountable hatred which, under the mask of friendship, waits only for the friend's death or misfortune to shower upon his head a hail of reproaches, advice, jeers, or regrets.

When I read the diary, I felt sure of its sincerity because of the pitiless way in which he exposed his own weaknesses and his own vices. The story of a human soul, though a small one, is as interesting and valuable as the story of a whole people, especially if the story of the soul comprises the observations of a mature mind on itself, and if it be not prompted by the

PREFACE

vainglorious desire to arouse interest and awake astonishment. Take Jean Jacques Rousseau's *Confessions*, for instance. They are faulty because he penned them to read to his friends.

Thus it may only be the wish to be useful which has induced me to publish these fragments of a diary that came into my hands by the hazard of a die. Although I have changed the names of the characters mentioned, all of them will probably recognize themselves. Perhaps, also, when they read they will be able to excuse behaviour for which they have never ceased to blame a man who, after all, did not share the customary philosophy of life. We can generally forgive what we have become able to understand.

I have published here only matters that concern Pechorin's experiences in the Caucasus. I still have a manuscript book in which he tells the whole story of his life. Some day this will be submitted to the judgment of the world, but at present there are various weighty reasons why I cannot publish it.

Maybe some of my readers will wish to know Pechorin's character. I answer: 'Consider the title of the book.' They will perhaps reply: 'But surely the title is ironical?'

I do not know.

TAMAN

TAMAN

TAMAN, in Caucasia on the eastern side of the Straits of Kertch between the Black Sea and the Sea of Azov, and therefore facing the Crimea, is one of the nastiest sea-coast towns in Russia. So it seems to me anyhow, for once I narrowly escaped dying of hunger there, and it was the place in which someone tried to drown me.

I arrived by mail-coach late one night. The driver reined in his team at the outskirts of the town, in front of the gates of the only stone house the place could boast. The sentry, a Black-Sea Cossack, hearing the bells, shouted fiercely: 'Who goes there?' A sergeant and a corporal came out. I told them that I, an officer travelling on public business, had to join a unit on active service, and that I should need quarters. The corporal conducted me into the town. Every hut at which we applied (I was accompanied by a Cossack as batman) was full to bursting. It was very cold, and I was frightfully tired, having had no proper sleep for three nights, so I began to lose my temper, and shouted at the corporal:

'Brigand that you are, find me a lodging

somewhere. I don't care a damn what sort of place it is, so long as I can sleep.'

'There's still one lodging left, Excellency,' said the corporal, scratching his head, 'but I don't think you'd like it, for it's frightfully dirty, and has a bad name.'

I did not understand what he meant by the last phrase, so I told him to go ahead and take me there. After wandering a long time through muddy lanes between ruinous fences, we reached a small hut within a stone's throw of the sea.

The moon, a couple of days past the full, was pouring its light upon the thatched roof and white-washed walls of what was to be my habitation. On the other side of the yard, which was surrounded by a wall of rough stones, was a second hut, smaller and more dilapidated than the first. These edifices were on a cliff, from the foot of which came the unceasing murmur of the waves. The moon looked quietly down upon the restless element which submits to her guidance, and by moonlight I could discern, far away seaward, two ships whose black rigging, like a spider's web, stood out motionless against the pallid horizon.

'Ships anchored there,' I said to myself. 'To-morrow I shall be able to set sail for Gelenjik.'

TAMAN

Telling the batman to go to the mail-coach for my trunk, and to settle accounts with the coachman, I knocked at the door of the hut, expecting the owner to appear. Not a sign or sound came in reply. I tried again. Still silence. What was the meaning of this? At last a boy of about fourteen crawled out of a shed I had scarcely noticed.

'Where's your master?'

'Haven't got a master.'

'What, no master at all?'

'None.'

'Where's your mistress, then?'

'Gone to the village.'

'Who will open the door for me?' I asked, giving it a kick.

At this it opened of itself, and a smell of damp emerged. Then I struck a match and thrust it close to the boy's nose, and on either side of it I saw white eyes. He was blind, had been blind from birth. He stood before me motionless while I examined his features closely.

Let me say at once that I have a strong prejudice against all who are blind, deformed or maimed, deaf and dumb, all who have lost an arm or a leg, or are otherwise mutilated. I have noticed that there is invariably a strange connexion between a man's outward appearance and his character, as if through losing a limb he had undergone some amputation of the mind.

It was with this conviction that I began to examine the blind boy's face, but what can one read in a face when the eyes are sightless? For a long time, therefore, I looked at him with a modicum of pity, when, of a sudden, a faint smile flickered on his thin lips, and (I can't explain why) this aroused in me a very disagreeable feeling. It led me to suspect that this lad was not so blind as he seemed. Vainly I tried to assure myself that those white eyes could not possibly be a fake—and, besides, what could the boy gain by such malingering? What was I to do? I quickly succumbed to my prejudice.

At length I asked him: 'Are you the son of the owner of this house?'

'No.'

'What are you, then?'

'An orphan and a pauper.'

'Has the mistress any children?'

'No. She had a daughter, but the girl ran away to sea with a Tartar.'

'What sort of Tartar?'

'The devil may know, I don't. I've heard he was a Crimean Tartar, a boatman from Kertch.'

I went into the hut. Its furniture consisted of two benches and a table, and a huge chest standing near the stove. There was not a single icon on the walls—a bad sign. The sea-wind was blowing in through a broken window-pane. Taking a candle-end out of my trunk, I lighted it, and began to unpack the other things. I put my sword and musket in a corner, my pistols on the table, and my cloak on a bench, while the Cossack batman (who had come back bringing the trunk) spread his cloak on the other, and we lay down to sleep. In ten minutes the good fellow was snoring, but I was not so lucky, being haunted in the darkness by the blind boy's white eyes. They kept me awake.

About an hour passed in this way. The moonlight was streaming through the window on to the earthen floor of the hut. Suddenly a shadow passed across the patch of moonlight on the floor. I sat up and looked out of the window. Someone passed it again, and vanished, God knows where. I could hardly suppose that he could have run down the precipice at the top of which the hut stood, and yet how else could he have disappeared so swiftly? I rose, put on a tunic, buckled my dagger round my waist, and went out of the hut as quietly as possible. Coming to meet me was the blind boy. I snuggled up against the wall, and he passed me unaware, walking firmly but carefully. Under one arm he was carrying a bundle, and, making for the harbour, he went swiftly down a narrow and precipitous path I had not previously noticed. 'Then the eyes of the blind shall be opened, and the ears of the deaf shall be unstopped,' I thought, as I followed him close enough to keep him in sight.

The moon, meanwhile, was being obscured by clouds, and the sea by a fog-bank, so that the stern-light of the nearest ship was barely visible, but on the shore the waves were breaking so high that from moment to moment I thought she might be swamped.

With difficulty I made my way down the dangerous path, at the foot of which the boy stopped for a moment and then turned to the right. He walked so close to the raging waters that it looked as though a wave would catch him and sweep him out to sea; but the confident way in which he stepped from rock to rock and avoided the holes between them, showed that this could not be the first time he had passed along here. Finally he halted, as if some noise had arrested his attention, and sat down on the ground with his bundle close at hand. Sheltering behind a stone buttress that projected from the cliff, I watched his every movement. In a few minutes the figure of someone clad in white appeared from the opposite direction. Whoever it was went up to the boy and sat down beside him. I was to leeward of them, and from time to time snatches of their conversation reached me.

'Well, blind boy,' said the new-arrival (it was a woman's voice), 'the storm is raging. Yanko won't come.'

'Yanko's not afraid of storms,' answered the other.

'The fog grows thicker,' rejoined the woman distressfully.

'That will make it easier for him to slip past the revenue officers' craft.'

'But what if he's drowned?'

'No matter. You'd have to go to church next Sunday without your new ribbon. That's all.'

There was silence for a time. I had already been struck by one fact. When the boy spoke to me he had a Little Russian accent, but he was now speaking with what we consider a 'proper' accent.

'You see I was right, after all,' broke in the boy suddenly, clapping his hands. 'Yanko is not afraid of the sea, or the wind, or fog, or a revenue cutter. Just listen. That noise is not made by the waves I am sure. It is the plash of his long sculls.'

TAMAN

The woman jumped up and began to peer uneasily into the distance.

'You're raving, blind boy,' she said. 'I can see nothing.'

Hard as I tried to glimpse the outlines of a boat in the distance, I also could see nothing.

Ten minutes went by, and then among the mountainous waves I made out a black dot, sometimes larger, sometimes smaller. It was a boat which rose slowly on to the crests of the waves, and then sank swiftly into the troughs between them, but steadily it approached the shore. The oarsman must be a bold fellow to venture across these fifteen miles of the straits on so stormy a night, and must have a powerful inducement to take the risks. Such were the thoughts with which—my heart beating violently—I looked at the wretched little craft. But she rode the rough waters as buoyantly as a duck, emerging from the abyss each time amid showers of spray with a great sweep of the oars. 'Now,' I thought, 'she will be swept ashore, and will be dashed to pieces'; but she skilfully made a half-turn and was washed unhurt up a little creek. Immediately there stepped out of her a man of middle height, wearing a Tartar sheepskin cap. He waved his hand to the others, who joined him, and all three proceeded to

TAMAN

drag something out of the boat. So heavily laden was she that I still find it impossible to understand how she can have kept afloat. Having each shouldered a load, they walked along the shore, where I soon lost sight of them. I thought it best to return to the hut, but the strange happenings had disturbed me so much that I was impatient for the morning.

When my Cossack awoke, he was very much surprised to see me fully dressed, but I did not tell him why it was so. I stood for some time at the window admiring the blue sky dotted with clouds, and the distant shore of Crimea—a lilac strip which ended in a rock on which a lighthouse stood. Then I went to Fort Fanagorya and asked the commandant how soon I could get a boat to Gelenjik.

Alas, he could tell me nothing definite. The ships in the harbour were either revenue cutters or vessels waiting for freight.

'Perhaps in three or four days the mail packet will arrive. Then we shall see.'

I returned to the hut bored and angry. My Cossack met me at the door. He looked in a blue funk.

'Things seem pretty bad, Excellency,' was his greeting.

'May be so, lad,' I answered. 'But God alone knows when we shall get away.'

This made him more alarmed than ever, and, coming close to me, he whispered:

'There's something wrong here. This morning I came across a Black-Sea sergeant who's an old acquaintance. We served together last year. When I told him where we were staying, he said: "Look here, comrade, that's a rotten place. The people who live there are up to no good."

'I wish I knew,'—the batman went on, 'what that blind boy does with himself. He goes everywhere quite alone, to the market, to fetch bread and get water. Evidently he's used to managing without help.'

'Never mind about him,' I said. 'Has the woman of the house turned up yet?'

'Yes, Excellency. While you were away the old woman came, and her daughter.'

'Her daughter? But she hasn't got a daughter.'

'Well, sir, I don't know who the girl can be, if she's not the old woman's daughter. Anyhow the old woman is now sitting in the hut.'

I went into the hovel to see. The stove was blazing hot, and she was cooking what seemed to me a big dinner for such poor people. I asked several questions, to each of which the crone returned the same answer, saying that she was too deaf to hear me. I could make nothing of her, so I tackled the blind boy who was sitting

TAMAN

in front of the stove and feeding it with chunks of wood.

'Now then, you little blind devil,' I said, pinching one of his ears, 'tell me where you went with that bundle last night.'

He began to shed tears and howl and wail. 'Where did I go? I didn't go anywhere. With a bundle? I had no bundle.'

The old woman could hear well enough now, and muttered. 'Of what are you accusing that poor afflicted boy? What harm has he done you?'

This put my dander up, and I went out, determined to solve the mystery.

Wrapping myself in my cloak I sat on a stone beside the wall of the enclosure, and stared into the distance. Immediately beneath was the sea, still raging after the storm of the night before, and the waves made a monotonous roar, like the hum of a sleeping town. It reminded me of vanished years, made me think of the north and of our frost-bound capital. Immersed in these memories, I forgot to notice the passage of time. Thus I spent an hour or more. Suddenly I heard a sound that resembled a song. Yes, it was a song, sung brightly by a woman. But where was she? I listened carefully. The singing was melodious—now long drawn out and sad; now brisk and lively. I looked round, but could see nobody. I listened again, and the sound seemed to come down from the sky. I raised my eyes. On the roof of the hut where I was lodging stood a girl in a striped dress, with her long hair unbound, so that she looked like a water-nymph. Shading her eyes from the sun with one hand, she was staring into the distance. She laughed and talked to herself, and then began singing again.

I remember every word of her song. Here it is:

> Towards the billowy freedom
> Of the green open sea
> Sails a multitude of ships.
>   White are their sails.
>
> And among all these ships
> Moves my own little boat;
> A boat which has no sails,
>   Only a pair of sculls.
>
> Fiercely the storm is raging,
> And the multitude of ships,
> Like birds spreading their wings,
>   Puts out to sea.
>
> To the sea I make obeisance,
> And say: 'O angry sea
> I pray thee work no harm
>   To my little boat;

TAMAN

For with things of great value
My little boat is freighted,
And through the night there guides her
A bold hand dear to me.'

Involuntarily I became aware that I had heard this voice overnight. I pondered for a minute, and when I next glanced at the roof the girl was no longer there. Suddenly she ran past me, singing another song, and, snapping her fingers, she went swiftly up to the old woman. The two began to quarrel. The old woman, in a fury, burst out laughing. Then I saw my Undine start bounding along in my direction. When she reached me she stopped and looked at me fixedly, as if surprised to see me there. A moment later she turned away indifferently, and quietly went down towards the harbour. But this was not the end. For all the rest of the day she kept passing my hut, never ceasing for a moment to sing and to bound.

She was a strange creature. In her face I could detect no signs of weakness of mind. On the contrary, her eyes always rested on me with piercing acuteness. Those eyes seemed equipped with some sort of magnetic power, and conveyed the idea that she was expecting to be questioned. Yet directly I began to talk, she ran away with a crafty smile.

TAMAN

Beyond doubt, I never saw another woman like her. She was by no means beautiful, though I must admit being prejudiced where beauty is concerned. Nevertheless she was thoroughbred —a thoroughbred among women, as among horses, being always notable. This is particularly obvious in the young women of France. Breeding shows itself especially in the hands and the feet; but the shape of the nose also signifies a great deal. A straight nose is a rare thing in Russia.

My songstress did not look more than eighteen. The things that seemed to me very remarkable about her were the unusual suppleness of her figure, her queer way of inclining her head to one side, her long auburn tresses, a golden tinge on the sunburned skin of her neck and shoulders, and especially the straightness of her nose—straight noses being (I repeat) exceptional in Russia. Though her glances at me were shifty, and I read in them traces of wildness and suspicion, and though there was something furtive in her smile—my weakness for straight noses is overwhelming, and I could not but fancy that I had happened upon Mignon, the mysterious Italian maiden in Goethe's *Wilhelm Meisters Lehrjahre*, a marvellous product of the German imagination. There were, in fact, many likenesses: the same swift change from intense restlessness to complete immobility, the same enigmatic remarks, the same bounding movements and strange songs. Towards evening I stopped her at the door, and the following conversation ensued.

'Tell me, pretty one,' I said, 'what you were doing on the roof today.'

'I was looking to see from what quarter the wind came.'

'What does that matter to you?'

'Happiness comes from the same quarter as the wind.'

'Do you fancy that your songs can attract happiness?'

'Where one sings, there one is happy.'

'Cannot you just as easily bring sorrow by singing?'

'Oh well, when things don't get better, they get worse; and there is very little distance between good and bad.'

'Who taught you that song?'

'No one taught me. I sing as the fancy takes me. Whoever listens wisely, will understand; but one who ought not to listen, will not understand.'

'What is your name, songstress?'

'He who christened me, knows.'

'Who christened you?'

'How can I tell?'

'You're a strange creature, but I've learned a little about you.'

Her expression did not change, and there was no quiver of her lips. She was as unconcerned as if I had been speaking of someone else. I went on:

'I know that you went down to the shore last night.'

In a grave tone, I described all I had seen, expecting to arouse consternation. Instead she burst out laughing.

'You may have seen a lot,' she said; 'but you know precious little. What you do know, you had better keep to yourself.'

'But suppose I think it my duty to report to the commandant?'

I said this seriously, and even in what might be called an official manner. She made a startled jump, began to sing, and hid herself like a bird one has scared out of the bushes. The question I had blurted was exceedingly foolish. I did not, at the moment, realize its importance, but later I had good reason for repenting it.

Darkness had fallen. I told the batman to boil the kettle as if we had been on active service, and while he was making tea I sat at the table smoking. Then, when I was finishing my second glass of tea, I heard the door creak, and there came the rustle of a dress and the sound of footsteps. I turned round. It was she, my Undine. She sat down opposite me without a word and looked me straight in the eyes. I don't know why I thought so, but her gaze seemed tender, reminding me of some of the glances which had influenced me greatly earlier in life. It was as if she were waiting to be questioned, but I remained silent, and was even considerably embarrassed. The pallor of her face betrayed emotion. One of her hands wandered aimlessly over the table, and I noticed that it trembled. She held her breath, too.

The comedy was beginning to bore me, and I resolved to end the silence by offering her a glass of tea, when suddenly she jumped up, flung her arms round my neck, and pressed her lips on mine in a burning kiss. My eyes darkened and my head swam. I tried to clasp her fervently and strongly, with the passion of youth, but she slipped from my embrace with the gliding movement of a snake, and whispered:

'Tonight, when they are all asleep, come down to the shore.'

In an instant she was out of the room, and as she hurried along the passage she knocked over the teapot and the candle, which were on the floor.

'A she-devil, that girl,' exclaimed the Cossack, who was lying on a heap of straw and had hoped to warm himself with what was left of the tea. This exclamation restored me to my senses.

Two hours later, when all was silent in the harbour, I awoke the batman and said to him:

'If I fire my pistol, you must make for the shore at top speed.'

He opened his eyes and said mechanically: 'Very good, Excellency.'

Having stuck a pistol in my belt, I went out. She was waiting for me at the top of the path, wearing a thin dress with a kerchief tied round her supple waist.

'Follow me,' she said, taking my hand, and thus we began the descent. I am puzzled to know why I didn't break my neck, but at the bottom we turned to the right along the way where I had followed the blind boy on the previous night. The moon had not yet risen, and only two stars were strong enough to shine like beacons in the misty sky. Big waves were breaking on the shore in regular succession, and the swell rocked the boat which was moored in the creek.

TAMAN

'We'll take this boat,' said my companion.

I shivered, having no taste for sentimental sea-trips, but I did not see my way to withdraw at this stage. She jumped aboard. I followed her, and I had hardly recovered my footing when I realized that we were under way.

'What's the meaning of this?' I angrily asked.

'It means that I love you,' she said, pressing me down on one of the seats and flinging her arms round me. She rubbed her cheek against mine, and I felt her hot breath on my face. Suddenly I heard a splash. Something had dropped into the water. I thrust my fingers into my belt. The pistol had gone! A terrible suspicion seized me, and the blood rushed to my head. I looked round. We must have been quite a hundred yards from the shore, and I could not swim. I tried to push her away, but she clung to my clothing like a cat, and gave me such a violent jerk that I almost fell overboard. The boat began to rock, but I righted her and the girl and I became engaged in a savage struggle. Rage gave me strength, but I soon realized that my antagonist was more than my equal in such an encounter.

'What do you want?' I shouted, crushing her little hands in mine. I heard her fingers crack, but she did not scream.

TAMAN

'You saw,' she answered, 'and you intend to report us.'

With superhuman energy she jammed me against the gunwale, and we both hung over the side so that her hair touched the water. This was the critical moment. Kneeling on the bottom boards, I clutched her hair with one hand, her throat with the other. She lost her grip of my clothing, and I managed to fling her into the water.

Dark though it was, I could see her head rise twice out of the sea; then she vanished, and I thought she was drowned.

In the boat I found a broken oar, and with this I managed to paddle back to the shore, where I made the painter fast.

Climbing up the path which led to the hut, almost unthinkingly I kept watch on the spot where, the night before, the girl and the blind boy had waited for the boatman. By now the moon had risen, and I fancied I could perceive something white on the shore. Being curious to see what was there, I crawled through the grass to the edge of the cliff. Stretching my head over it, I found I could make out almost everything that was going on below. I was not very much surprised, and was even a little glad to catch sight of my water-nymph. She was wringing the

TAMAN

sea-water out of her long hair, while her wet dress clung to her supple figure and swelling bosom. Soon a boat showed up in the offing and rapidly approached the shore. Out of it, just as before, stepped a man wearing a Tartar cap, but his hair was cut in the Cossack fashion, and he had a big dagger in a sheath strapped to his waist.

'Yanko,' she said, 'the game's up.'

Then they had a long conversation, but in such low tones that I could hear nothing. At length, speaking louder, Yanko said:

'But where's the blind boy?'

'I sent him to fetch some stuff,' she replied.

In a few minutes he appeared, stooping beneath a sack, which he flung into the boat.

'Listen, blind boy,' said Yanko. 'Keep a sharp eye on the place where the valuable goods are —you know; and tell' (I couldn't catch the name) 'that I shall no longer work for him. Things are turning out badly, and he won't see me again. It's too risky here, so I shall look for a job elsewhere. But I know he'll not find another chap so smart as I am. You can tell him, too, that if he'd not been so close-fisted, Yanko would never have left him in the lurch. I shall get something to do in any place where the wind blows or the sea roars.'

After a minute or two's silence, the smuggler resumed, waving a hand towards the girl:

'She's coming with me; not safe for her here. As for the old woman, tell her—more or less—that her day is done. She's lived her life, and the time has come for her to die. Anyhow, she won't see me again.'

'But what's to become of me?' asked the blind boy, plaintively.

'That's no concern of mine,' answered Yanko.

Meanwhile my Undine had jumped on board the boat and was beckoning her comrade. Yanko slipped a coin or two into the boy's hand, saying:

'Here's something to buy gingerbread with.'

'Is that all?' asked the recipient.

'Well, here's some more,' answered the smuggler; but this time the coins fell, for I heard them ring against the shingle, and the blind boy did not even stoop to look for them.

Yanko sat down in the boat. The wind was blowing off shore. He hoisted a small sail, and was quickly making out to sea. The white sail in the moonlight stood out in relief against the dark waves. The boy was sitting on the shore, and I heard a sad sound. He was crying bitterly, and went on sobbing for a long time.

I was profoundly depressed, as I stood on the edge of the cliff wondering why fate had involved me with this band of smugglers, who were decent enough after their fashion. Like a stone dropped into a well, I had troubled their peace—and, like such a stone, I had nearly gone to the bottom.

I went back to the hut. In the passage a candle-end flickered on a wooden dish. Orders notwithstanding, my Cossack was sound asleep, though he was grasping his musket with both hands. Not troubling him, I took the candle and went inside. Alas my box, my sword chased with silver, the Daghestan dagger a friend had given me—all, all, had vanished. It was easy to guess what that accursed boy had been carrying in the sack. I awoke the batman roughly enough with a shake, and gave him a tongue-lashing. But things were past mending. I should only have made a fool of myself by complaining to the authorities that a blind boy had robbed me, and that a girl of eighteen had nearly succeeded in drowning me. In the morning, thanks be, I was able to clear out, and I said goodbye to Taman.

I don't know what happened to the old woman and the blind boy.

But why on earth should I, an officer travelling on service, have got mixed up with the joys and sorrows of such a crew?

PRINCESS MARY

PRINCESS MARY

May 11th. Yesterday I reached Pyatigorsk, and found rooms just inside the town on high ground at the foot of Mashuk. If rough weather comes, the clouds will lap my roof. When I opened the window at five o'clock this morning, the room was filled with the scent of flowers that were growing in the little front garden. Branches of cherry blossom peer in at the window, and the wind sometimes scatters the white petals over my writing-table. The view in three directions is splendid. Westward are the five blue peaks of Beshtu, looking (to quote Pushkin) like the vestiges of a scattered thunderstorm. To the north the horizon is blocked by Mashuk, which resembles a Persian fur-cap. The eastern prospect is comparatively gentle, for below me here lies the clean, new-built town, from which rise the murmur of the medicinal springs and the voices of the cosmopolitan crowd. Beyond, the hills, blue and hazy in the distance, form an amphitheatre, fringed by the silvery chain of the snows that stretch from Mount Kazbek to the twin summits of Elbruz.

It is delightful to live in such a place. An

agreeable feeling pervades my whole body. The air is as pure and fresh as a child's kiss. The sun shines brightly, and there is not a cloud to dim the sky. Could anyone want more? There seems no place for passions, longings, or regrets. But it's time for me to go out. I have to drink the waters at the Elizabeth Spring, where I am told the visitors forgather in the morning.

On my way to the middle of the town, along the boulevard, I met several groups of pedestrians, walking slowly up the hill. Mostly they were the families of landowners from the steppes. This was obvious from the threadbare, old-fashioned coats of the men, and because their wives and daughters were overdressed. Plainly the men were acquainted with every young fellow they were in the habit of meeting, for they scanned me curiously. The fact that my coat had a St. Petersburg cut misled them, but as soon as they perceived that I was wearing military epaulets, their expression grew irritated.

The women of the locality, the hostesses of the spa (so to say), were less ungracious, being used in the Caucasus to find that passionate hearts could beat beneath regimental buttons, and that intelligent brains were covered by white forage caps. These ladies were, indeed, most amiable, and had been so for a long time. Each year fresh admirers took the place of the old, which perhaps accounted for their persistent kindliness.

While walking up the narrow path that leads to the Elizabeth Spring, I overtook and outstripped a lot of civilians and soldiers who, as I learned afterwards, form a special category of the persons that come for the hydropathic treatment which is far-famed. They drink freely—but not the waters; take very little exercise; make love only as an occasional pastime; often gamble; and in general complain of boredom. They put on airs; for instance, when dipping a glass into the sulphur spring they assume an academic pose. The civilians sport light-blue neckties, while the soldiers' heads seem to emerge with difficulty from collars that are much too high. They profess a great contempt for the provincial ladies, and sigh for the aristocratic salons of the capital (to which they have never been admitted).

At last I got to the spring. In the little square nearby were the red-roofed bathhouse and a covered gallery where visitors could walk under shelter when it was raining. A few wounded officers sat on benches. They had crutches beside them, and looked both pale and unhappy. Some lady patients were walking briskly up and down the square, hoping to intensify the effect of the waters. Two or three of them were quite good-looking. In the alleys which lead through the vineyards on the lower slopes of Mashuk I caught sight of ladies who obviously had a preference for male companionship, since the other member of each of these couples wore a military cap or an ugly billycock. On a steep rock was a belvedere called the Aeolian Harp, where sat people fond of views, and scanning Elbruz through telescopes. Among them were two tutors in charge of pups who had been sent to Pyatigorsk for the cure of scrofula.

Being out of breath, I stopped at the foot of the hill and, leaning against a corner of the belvedere, I studied the picturesque prospect. Then a familiar voice hailed me:

'Hullo, Pechorin, how long have you been here?'

I turned round to greet Grushnitsky, whose acquaintance I had made at the fighting-front. Having received a bullet wound in the leg, he had come to take the waters a week ago.

He was a cadet who had only been a year in the service. By a peculiar affectation, he wore a private's thick cloak, and he had been honoured by the bestowal of the St. George's Cross. Well-built, dark, and with black hair, he looked twenty-five, though he was really four years younger. A man with a trick of flinging his head back as he talked, he now continually tugged at his moustache with his left hand, the right hand being occupied with a crutch. He spoke quickly and affectedly, being one of those who have high-falutin phrases which they consider appropriate for every contingency, while they have no appreciation of beauty unadorned. Pompously they feign unusual emotions, sublime passions, and exceptional suffering. They love to produce an effect, and romantically minded provincial girls are apt to adore them. As they approach middle age, they may become respectable country gentlemen or else take to drink, or even aspire to both vocations. Such men may have excellent qualities, but they never have a poetic vein.

Grushnitsky's foible was for declamation. His words would pour forth in a flood directly the talk transgressed the limits of the conventional, and I found it impossible to argue with him. He did not answer objections, for he never listened to a word one said. The moment I stopped talking he would start a new tirade, ostensibly bearing on what I had been saying, but really nothing more than the continuation of his original argument.

He was far from being dull-witted. His epigrams were often amusing, though not pointed or spiteful. Never did he slay a man with a word. He did not know people and their weak sides, being exclusively concerned with his own life. His object was to become a hero of romance. So often had he endeavoured to convince others that he was not really created for this world, and was a prey to secret sufferings, that in the end he had almost come to believe as much himself. That was why he was so fond of wearing his thick cloak made for a ranker. I saw through him, and for this reason he did not like me, though to outward seeming we were on most friendly terms. By repute he was a very brave soldier. I had seen him in action. He brandished his sword, shouted, and blinked in a way that did not really betoken Russian courage.

Nor do I care for him. I have a feeling that some day we shall encounter one another on a narrow path, and that then one of us will come off badly.

His visit to Caucasia was likewise the upshot of his fanatical romanticism. I am confident that the day before he left his father's house he must have said, with a melancholy visage, to a fair lady, one of his neighbours, not simply that he was going on active service, but was going to his death, for . . . Here he would have covered his eyes with his hand, and said: 'No, you shall' (or 'thou shalt') 'never know the reason. Your pure soul would shrink from it. Why should I tell you? What am I to you? Do you understand me now?' And so on, and so forth.

He himself assured me that his purpose in joining the K—— regiment was to remain for ever a secret between him and heaven.

In other respects, when he threw off his tragic mantle Grushnitsky was a pleasant and amusing fellow enough. I was curious to see him with women, for I fancied that in their company he would show his peculiarities to the full.

We now met, of course, as old acquaintances. I began by asking him how people passed their time at the spa, and who were the most interesting among the visitors.

'Life here is rather trivial,' he said with a sigh. 'Those who drink the waters in the morning are as dull as invalids in general, and those who drink wine in the evening are as insufferable as most other healthy specimens of our race. There are some women here, but they are of very little interest. They play whist, dress badly, and their French is abominable. The only ones from

Moscow are Princess Ligovsky and her daughter, but I haven't made their acquaintance. People give me the go-by because I wear a private's cloak. The interest which it arouses has its seamy side—like alms-giving.'

As he was speaking, the ladies passed us on their way to the spring. One was well up in years, the other young and graceful. Their hats hid their faces, but their dresses were most fashionable. Nothing redundant in the way of flounces and furbelows. The younger wore a pearl-grey gown and had a light silk wrap round her slender shoulders. Her boots, of a puce tint, fitted closely round her thin ankles, and she was so agreeable to contemplate that even a man knowing little about the secrets of beauty would have been moved to gasp with admiration. Her gait, easy but high-bred, had an indefinable but unmistakable charm. As she went by I perceived a delicate perfume, such as clings sometimes to a beautiful woman's letter.

'That's Princess Ligovsky,' said Grushnitsky, 'and the girl is her daughter Mary, named after the English fashion. They've been here only three days.'

'But you've learned who they are already?'

'Oh, yes, I chanced to find out,' he answered, blushing. 'Yet I've no wish to make their acquain-

PRINCESS MARY

tance. Those swells look upon us poor soldiers as if we were wild beasts. What do they care if a forage cap covers a good brain, or a thick cloak a good heart?'

'Poor cloak,' I replied, smiling. 'But tell me, who is the man who has just come up to them and is offering them a glass so politely?'

'Oh, that's Raevich from Moscow, a dandy and a gambler. Look at the huge gold watch-chain which runs across his blue waistcoat. That great walking-stick might have suited Robinson Crusoe. His beard is in keeping, too; or would have done for a gardener.'

'You talk as if you hated the whole human race.'

'Well, so I do.'

'But why?'

At this moment the ladies left the spring and were passing close to us once more. Grushnitsky struck a theatrical attitude, supplemented with the aid of his crutch, and loudly replied in excellent French.

'My dear fellow, I hate human beings in preference to despising them. The latter would make life too detestable a farce.'

The pretty young princess looked fixedly and inquisitively at the man who had thus declaimed. The meaning of her glance was not obvious, but she was certainly not regarding him with derision, so in my inmost self I could not but congratulate him.

'That little princess is lovely,' I said to him. 'She has such velvety eyes. Yes, velvety. I advise you to use that word if you speak to anyone about her eyes. The upper and lower lashes are so long that the sunlight is not reflected from her pupils. I am very fond of eyes that don't gleam, but are so soft that they appear to caress one. The rest of her face is very fine as well. Have you noticed whether her teeth are really white? That's a most important feature. What a pity she did not smile at your spirited phrase.'

'You are talking of a beautiful woman as you might speak of the points of a thoroughbred mare imported from England,' replied Grushnitsky with considerable irritation.

'My dear fellow,' I answered, speaking French with (I think) a passable imitation of his accent as well as his words: 'I despise women in preference to loving them. The latter would make life too absurd a melodrama.'

Turning away I left him. For half an hour I walked along the alleys of the vineyard, among limestone crags overgrown with bushes. Then, since it was getting hot, I made for my rooms. But as I passed the sulphur spring, I halted in

PRINCESS MARY

the pergola, hoping to cool off in the shade, and here I witnessed a curious scene. Let me explain how the persons of the drama were placed. The princess and the Moscow dandy were sitting on a bench, engaged in earnest conversation. The young lady had apparently finished her last glass of the waters and was strolling thoughtfully up and down near the spring. Grushnitsky was standing still closer to the fountain. There was no one else within sight.

Going nearer, I took cover in a corner of the pergola. At this moment Grushnitsky dropped his glass on the sand, and tried hard to pick it up, but did not succeed for his wounded leg hindered him. The poor chap did his utmost, leaning on his crutch, but his efforts were futile. On his expressive face one could read that he was really suffering.

Princess Mary could see the difficulty even better than I.

She ran as lightly as a bird, stooped, picked up the glass, and handed it to him with a graceful movement, bowing courteously. Then she blushed, as she looked along the pergola. But when she realized that her mother had noticed nothing, she promptly regained composure. Before Grushnitsky had time to thank her, she was far away. A minute later she left the gallery with

PRINCESS MARY

her mother and the dandy, and, as she passed Grushnitsky, she glanced at him with dignity and decorum, barely turning her head. Indeed she did not even notice the look of passionate gratitude with which he favoured her, following her with his eyes until she reached the foot of the hill and was lost to sight among the lime trees of the boulevard. Not quite lost, though, since I could see her hat moving along the street, until she entered the gate of one of the finest houses in Pyatigorsk. Her mother followed her in, having said goodbye to Raevich.

Only then did the love-lorn cadet notice that I was there.

'Did you see?' he asked, grasping my hand. 'She's an angel.'

'What makes you say that?' I replied, with an assumption of absolute unconcern.

'But didn't you notice?'

'Oh, yes, I saw her pick up your glass. Had the attendant been on hand, he would have done the same thing, rather more quickly, hoping to earn a tip. It was plain enough why she was sorry for you. You made such a woeful face when you were trying to bend your wounded leg.'

'Didn't it touch you to see her soul shine through her face?'

PRINCESS MARY

'No, not particularly.'

I was lying, of course, because I wanted to annoy him. With me the passion for contradiction is ingrained. All my life has been spent in weary and vain attempts to withstand my heart or my judgment. The presence of an enthusiast makes me as cold as ice, while I think I should become passionately excited if I had much to do with a dull and phlegmatic person. Let me also admit that another feeling, unpleasant but by no means unfamiliar, had taken possession of me—jealousy. I confess this because it is my habit to acknowledge everything, to myself at least. Moreover I doubt whether any young man, having come across a pretty woman, and had his attention attracted to her, could readily bear seeing her, suddenly and conspicuously, single out a possible rival. Anyone who had lived in the great world and had his vanity tickled would have been jealous in similar circumstances.

Without saying more, I walked down hill and along the boulevard beside Grushnitsky. We passed the windows of the house where our young princess was concealed. No, not concealed, for there she was, sitting at a window. Clutching me by the arm, Grushnitsky flung her one of those mysteriously tender looks which have so little effect on women. Raising my lorgnette, I could make out that she smiled at my companion, and was also annoyed by my use of the quizzing-glasses. How, indeed, could an officer in the Caucasus dare, without introduction, to scrutinize a Moscow beauty in such a way?

May 13th. This morning the doctor paid me a visit. His name is Werner, but he is a Russian right enough. Nothing to be surprised at. I used to know a man called Ivanoff, who was a German.

Werner is a remarkable man in many respects. Like most members of his profession he is a sceptic and a materialist; but he is also a poet, and a good one. Though he has never written a line of poetry, he is a poet in his behaviour and often in his words. He has studied all the strings of the human heart, like the nerves of a 'subject' in the dissecting-room, but he has never been able to turn his knowledge to account, any more than a skilled pathologist can always cure a fever. Usually Werner laughs on the quiet at his patients, but I once saw him shed tears over a dying soldier.

He was a poor man who dreamed of what he could do with millions, though he would not have moved a step to gain money. Indeed he once told me that he would rather do a good turn to an enemy than a friend, since by helping a friend he would be selling his kindness, whereas by helping an enemy he would probably intensify the latter's hatred. He had a sharp tongue, and from an epigram of his more than one excellent fellow had come to be considered a fool. His competitors, other medicos at the spa who were jealous of him, spread a report that he was wont to draw caricatures of his patients, most of whom, thereupon, immediately losing their tempers, dispensed with his services. His friends, who amounted to all the decent men serving in the Caucasus, did their best to sustain his diminishing credit.

On those who judge by first impressions, his appearance produced an unfavourable effect, which did not last in persons whose eyes were competent to read the signs of a well-tried and aspiring soul. Women sometimes love such men to distraction, and would not exchange their homely features for the beauty of an Endymion. Let us do justice to women. Numbers of them have an instinctive appreciation of spiritual beauty. Perhaps that is why men like Werner love women so passionately.

He was of small stature, thin, and feeble as a

child. Like Byron, he had one leg shorter than the other. In comparison with his body, his head was enormous. His hair was cropped very short, and this disclosed 'bumps' in his skull which a phrenologist would have considered to denote most contradictory tendencies. His small, dark eyes were incessantly moving, for he was trying to read people's thoughts. He dressed tastefully and neatly, keeping his small, sinewy hands covered with lemon-coloured gloves, whereas his frock-coat, waistcoat, and necktie were invariably black. Young fellows were wont to speak of him as 'Mephisto', and he professed irritation at this nickname, though really it tickled his vanity.

He and I soon learned to understand one another and became fairly close friends, though I am little inclined for friendship, considering that of two friends one is always the other's slave, though usually neither of them will admit as much. I cannot bear to be anyone's slave, but consider that to be master is almost as troublesome, for it involves unceasing deceit. Besides, I have a servant, and am well off.

Let me explain, however, the way in which Werner and I got acquainted. I met him at S——, among a big, noisy crowd of young men. Towards the close of the evening the conversation took a metaphysical turn, when the members of the company began to talk about their convictions, differing in each case.

'So far as I am concerned,' said the doctor, 'I have only one conviction.'

'What is it?' I asked, since this was the first time Werner had spoken.

'I am positively assured that, sooner or later, one fine morning, I shall die.'

'Well, I have two convictions, so I am richer than you,' I replied, 'being likewise certain that one loathsome evening I had the misfortune to be born.'

All the others thought that we were talking nonsense, though really not one of them had uttered anything pithier. From that moment Werner and I were drawn together. We moved apart from the others, to talk seriously about a number of abstract topics, until we both became aware that each of us was humbugging. Thereupon we looked significantly at one another as (according to Cicero) the Roman augurs used to do. Then we burst out laughing, and parted, well pleased with our evening.

When Werner came into my study this morning, I was lying on the sofa as I stared at the ceiling with my hands clasped behind my head. Having leaned his stick against the wall in a corner, he sat down in the armchair, yawned, and said it was getting very hot out-of-doors. When I had replied that the flies were a damned nuisance, we both lapsed into silence for a while.

At length I said: 'My dear Doctor, the world would be a dull place if there weren't any fools in it. Still, we are both wise men, since we know beforehand that we might go on quarrelling about this and that for ever and ever—so we don't quarrel. We know, too, nearly all one another's innermost thoughts. One word suffices to tell us the whole story. Through triple wrappings, each of us can see to the very bottom of the other's feelings. What is sad seems to us ridiculous, and what is funny seems sad, though substantially we are indifferent to most things. In fact, since we know one another through and through, we can't hide anything. All that remains to us is to talk about something new. Tell me something new.'

Being tired by my long speech, I shut my eyes and yawned.

After brief reflection, he answered: 'There is an idea, after all, in that gibberish of yours.'

'Two ideas, at least,' I protested.

'Well, if you tell me one, I'll tell you the other.'

PRINCESS MARY

'Very good, fire away,' I rejoined, still looking up at the ceiling, and smiling to myself.

'You want information about certain persons who have come here to drink the waters, and I can guess the names of those in whom you are interested, since they have already asked me about you.'

'Doctor, there is certainly no need for us to talk to one another, since we can read one another's minds.'

'Well, what's the second idea?'

'Here it is. I want to make you tell me something: first, because to listen is not so tiring as to talk; secondly, because I want to avoid making a mistake; thirdly, because in this way I may discover somebody else's secret; fourthly, because such clever persons as you like listeners better than talkers. Now I shall come to the core of the matter. What did Princess Ligovsky say about me?'

'You're sure it was Princess Ligovsky, and not her daughter Mary?'

'Absolutely certain.'

'Why?'

'Because the person Princess Mary asked you about was Grushnitsky.'

'You have a talent for sound inferences. Princess Mary said she was confident that the young man in a private's cloak must have been degraded to the ranks for fighting a duel.'

'I hope you left her in that agreeable delusion?'

'Of course I did.'

'There's some complication here,' I exclaimed in great delight. 'It will be of interest to us to unravel the plot of the comedy. Evidently the fates have decided that I am not to be bored.'

'I have a feeling,' said Werner, 'that poor Grushnitsky is going to be your victim.'

'Tell me some more, Doctor.'

'Princess Ligovsky said your face was familiar to her. I remarked that she had probably met you at some social gathering in St. Petersburg, and told her your name, which she knew. Your life there seems to have made a good deal of stir. The princess began to talk about your exploits, probably adding some contributions of her own to current gossip. Mary was keenly attentive, since for her you were presented as the hero of a novel in the latest style. I did not contradict the mother, though I knew she must be romancing for the most part.'

'You're a true friend,' I said, holding out my hand. He shook it warmly, and went on:

'If you like, I'll introduce you.'

'Thanks awfully,' I answered. 'But does one

PRINCESS MARY

introduce heroes? Should a hero become known in any other way than by saving his beloved from the jaws of death?'

'Do you really want to make love to Princess Mary?'

'Not in the least. But Doctor, I've gained a point at last, for you don't understand me without my telling you. Besides, I'm very sorry indeed,' I went on after a minute's pause. 'Never do I disclose my secrets. I like people to guess them for then I can deny them if necessary. But you must tell me something about mother and daughter. What sort of people are they?'

'The mother,' replied Werner, 'is about forty-five, and has an excellent digestion, but her blood is out of order, and that gives her red blotches on the cheeks. During the latter half of her life she has lived in Moscow, where, being sedentary, she has grown rather stout. She is fond of listening to spicy anecdotes, and when her daughter is out of the room she herself sometimes says things that are rather risky. She told me that Mary was as innocent as a dove. What concern was that of mine? I should have liked to tell her that she could be quite easy in her mind, for of course I would not repeat anything she said to me. Princess Ligovsky is being treated here for rheumatism; Princess Mary, for God knows what. I have told them both to drink two glasses of the waters every day, and to take the baths, not too strong, twice a week. The elder princess, it seems, is not unduly authoritative. She has a great respect for the intelligence and acquirements of her daughter, who can read Byron in the original and has studied algebra. At Moscow, I understand, young ladies go in for higher education. A very good move, in my opinion. Our men, as a rule, are such unamiable creatures, that being made love to by them must be repugnant to an intelligent woman. The mother is very fond of young men, but the daughter thinks them poor stuff. Such is the way in Moscow, where a girl is only interested in men of middle age.'

'Have you ever been in Moscow, Doctor?'
'Oh yes, I practised there for a time.'
'Well, go on.'
'I fancy I've told you all. No, there's one thing more. Princess Mary, it seems, is fond of talking about emotions, and what not. She has spent one winter in St. Petersburg, and didn't like it, especially the society life there. I expect she had a rather cold reception.'

'Was there anyone else visiting them when you saw them today?'

'Yes, an aide-de-camp, and a well-mannered

guardsman; also a newly-arrived lady, a connexion by marriage of Princess Ligovsky—must have been very good-looking before she got so ill. You may have seen her at the wells. Middle-height, a blonde with regular features but the face of a consumptive. A black mole on her right cheek. Her face is very striking.'

'A mole,' I muttered. 'Really a mole?'

Werner looked hard at me, stretched out his hand and laid it on my heart. 'My trick,' he said triumphantly. 'You know her.' In fact my heart was palpitating.

'Yes, it is indeed your trick this time. But I trust you. You won't betray me. I haven't seen her here, but your portrait enables me to recognize a woman with whom I fell in love a good while ago. Don't say a word to her about me, unless she actually asks you. Then say something disagreeable.'

'As you please,' answered the doctor, with a shrug.

When he had gone, I was seized with a fit of the blues. Had chance brought her back to the Caucasus, or had she come expressly in order to meet me? And how should we meet? Was it she, after all? My forebodings have never deceived me. No other man has ever lived whose past has had such power over him as mine has had over

PRINCESS MARY

me. The memory of suffering or of joy plucks painfully at the strings of my mind and invariably evokes the same note. I am so badly constructed that I can forget nothing, nothing.

At six o'clock after dinner, I went out on to the boulevard, which was thronged. The princesses, mother and daughter, were seated on a bench, surrounded by young men who were paying them attention. Sitting down on another bench at a little distance, I stopped two dragoon officers with whom I was acquainted and began telling them a story. It must certainly have been a funny one, for they laughed uproariously. Curiosity attracted some members of the princesses' circle, and thus it went on until in a little while they had all joined my group. I continued talking. My stories were idiotically amusing, and my comments upon the freaks who passed by were actively malicious. I entertained my hearers till sunset. Occasionally the mother and the daughter walked by arm-in-arm, accompanied by an old cripple. Princess Mary's glance, as it lit on me, expressed vexation, which she tried to mask with assumed indifference.

'What was he talking to you about?' she asked one of the young men, who had rejoined her from politeness. 'He must have been telling a

PRINCESS MARY

most interesting story. Did it concern his experiences at the front?' This was said in a loud tone, and implied criticism which was intended to reach my ears.

'Aha,' I thought. 'You're thoroughly annoyed. Wait a bit, till you see what happens.'

Grushnitsky followed her like a beast of prey, never losing sight of her. I bet that he will ask someone tomorrow to introduce him to the mother, who will be very glad since she is feeling bored.

May 16th. During the last two days my affairs have greatly advanced. Beyond question, Princess Mary detests me. Her friends have already repeated to me several epigrams she has uttered on my account, caustic enough, but also very flattering. She finds it exceedingly strange that I, who am accustomed to good society and am well acquainted with her cousins and aunts in St. Petersburg, should not try to make her acquaintance. Every day we encounter one another at the spring or on the boulevard, but I have made no move in her direction; I do my utmost to detach her admirers—dazzling aides-de-camp, distinguished young men, etc.—and I seldom fail. I have always disliked entertaining guests in my own rooms, but now the place is crowded with men who take their meals with me, dining, supping, and gambling. My champagne obviously triumphs over the magnetic power of her eyes.

Yesterday I met her when I went into Chelahoff's shop, where she was bargaining for a lovely Persian rug. She implored her mother not to grudge a long price, because the rug would greatly adorn her boudoir. I outbid her by forty roubles, bought the thing, and was rewarded by a glance of the utmost fury. Towards dinner time I had my Circassian charger, decked with the rug, led past her window. Werner was with the Ligovsky's when this happened, and he told me that the effect was dramatic. I gather that she has declared war against me. Certainly two of the aides-de-camp are very cool in their greetings, though both men dine with me every day.

Grushnitsky looks mysterious. He walks with his hands clasped behind his back and never greets anybody. His wounded leg has suddenly got better, so that he hardly limps. He has found opportunities for entering into conversation with Princess Ligovsky, and for paying her daughter a compliment. Princess Mary, it is plain, has but little discretion, for since then she has answered his salutations with a cordial smile.

PRINCESS MARY

'You really don't want to become acquainted with the Ligovskys?' he asked me yesterday.

'Really not.'

'But you might bear in mind that theirs is the pleasantest house in the spa. You'll find all the best people of the neighbourhood there.'

'My friend, the "best people" bore me stiff, whether they are of the neighbourhood or not. Besides, do you visit them yourself?'

'No, I haven't called yet. I've exchanged words with them two or three times, that's all. I can hardly bring myself to fish for an invitation, though that is often done here. It would be different if I were a fully commissioned officer, and entitled to wear epaulets.'

'I don't agree. You're all the more interesting because you haven't so far got your commission. You don't know how to derive the best advantage from a favourable situation. A sensitive young lady cannot but feel that since you wear a private's cloak you must be something between a hero and a martyr.'

Grushnitsky smiled with gratification, but thought it proper to say 'Oh, nonsense.'

'I am certain,' I went on, 'that Princess Mary is already in love with you.'

He blushed up to the ears, and put on an offended air.

PRINCESS MARY

Vanity, you are the fulcrum of the lever with which Archimedes could have moved the world!

'You can take nothing seriously,' he replied, feigning anger. 'Remember she hardly knows me.'

'Women only love men they don't know.'

'Nor do I honestly want to please her. I should merely like to gain admission into a very pleasant house, and it would be presumptuous of me to hope for anything more. If you were in question, matters would be different. St. Petersburg conquerors have merely to look at a woman and she melts. But you probably don't know, Pechorin, what the young princess said of you.'

'Has she been talking about me already?'

'Don't prepare to rejoice. By chance I exchanged a few remarks with her at the spring, and one of the first things she said was: "Who is the gentleman with the heavy, disagreeable look? I mean the one who was with you when. . . ." She broke off and blushed, being obviously reluctant to mention the day when she was so kind to me. "Don't trouble to say when," I interposed. "I am not likely to forget."—You see I can't congratulate you, Pechorin. You are in her bad books. It's a pity, for Mary is charming.'

Let me say in passing that Grushnitsky is one of those men who have a trick of saying 'My

Mary' or 'My Sophia', as the case may be, about women with whom they have no more than a trifling acquaintance. Enough that they should believe themselves to have made a good impression upon the fair ones.

Looking grave, I said to him:

'I agree that her appearance is worth noting. But you'd better watch out, Grushnitsky. Russian girls are apt to care only for platonic love, which will not involve marriage, and, believe me, platonic love is a very fatiguing business. Apparently Princess Mary is one of the women who look mainly for amusement, and if you should bore her in the least you will no longer have a chance. Your silence must arouse her curiosity, while your conversation should never satisfy her to the full. You ought to keep her uneasy without pause. For your sake she will disregard public opinion ten or a dozen times, will consider this a sacrifice, and to repay herself will begin tormenting you. Then she will only say that she can't endure you. Unless you gain a real hold on her, your first kiss will not give you any right to a second. She will flirt with you ad lib., and a couple of years afterwards will marry some hideous wretch in deference to her mother's wishes, while persuading herself that she is desperately unfortunate, having never loved but one man—you, of course. It was the will of heaven that she should not wed you, a man who wore a ranker's cloak, though undoubtedly beneath that thick grey cloak a passionate and noble heart must have been beating.'

Grushnitsky banged the table with his fist and began to stride up and down the room.

I laughed to myself, and even smiled openly once or twice, but luckily he paid no attention to this. Obviously he was in love, for he was more credulous than ever. He even turned up one day carrying a little leather case such as is used for holding a ring. When he had gone out of the room leaving it on the table for a moment, I took the liberty of opening it. Yes, it contained a ring of local manufacture, silver with black inlay of enamel, and inside was engraved the name 'Mary', and also the date on which she had picked up the famous glass for him. I have kept my own counsel about this discovery, not wishing to force an avowal. I should prefer him to confide in me spontaneously. It will probably be most amusing.

It was late this morning when I got up and went to the spring. Nobody about. The heat was oppressive. White streamers of cloud were

PRINCESS MARY

stretching down wind from the snowy peaks, and seemed to herald a thunderstorm. Mashuk was smoking like a torch whose flame has just been extinguished. The serpentine tufts of vapour might have been entangled by the thorn bushes that covered the slopes—or thus it appeared. The atmosphere was charged with electricity. Feeling profoundly miserable, I plunged into a vine alley that led to a grotto, my mind concentrated on the young woman with the mole on her cheek, the woman Werner had spoken of. Why was she here? Was it really the one with whom I had been in love? What ground had I for thinking so? There are plenty of women with birthmarks on the cheek. Yet I was convinced that there could be no mistake, as I entered the grotto. Here it was comparatively dark and cool, but when I looked about I could see that there was a woman seated on a stone bench. She wore a black shawl, and a straw hat which hid her face, since her head was bent forward. I was about to withdraw, lest I should disturb her reverie, when she looked up at me.

'Vera,' I involuntarily exclaimed.

She trembled and turned pale.

'I knew that you were here,' she said.

Sitting beside her, I took her hand. A long-forgotten thrill ran through me at the sound of her dear voice. She looked at me with eyes which were deep and quiet, but conveyed a glimmer of mistrust and something like reproach.

'It is long since we last saw one another,' I murmured.

'Very long,' she replied, 'and much has changed for us both.'

'Does that mean that you no longer love me?'

'I am married,' she answered.

'Again? But you were married when we met a few years ago, and that did not prevent. . . .'

She snatched away her hand, and her cheeks flamed.

'Perhaps you love your second husband?'

She said nothing, and turned her face aside.

'Or he may be very jealous?'

Still silence.

'What is it? Is he young, handsome, rich? Or are you afraid of him?'

Glancing at her, I was much moved, for her face showed despair, and her eyes were brimming over with tears.

'Tell me,' she whispered at last. 'Do you enjoy torturing me? It is so long since I saw you. From the time of our first meeting, you have brought me nothing but suffering.'

PRINCESS MARY

Her voice was breaking as she leaned towards me and rested her head on my breast.

'Perhaps that is true,' I thought. 'It may explain why you loved me. Joy can be forgotten, but pain never.'

I drew her close to me, and thus we remained for a considerable time. At last our lips were joined in a passionate kiss. Her hands were cold as ice, but her head was burning. Then we began one of those conversations whose thoughts cannot be conveyed in black upon white, and which, indeed, it is impossible to remember. As in an Italian opera, the sound is more important than the sense.

She was decisively opposed to my making her husband's acquaintance. He was a lame old man whom I had caught sight of on the boulevard. She had married him for her son's sake. He was rich and suffered from rheumatism. But I restrained myself from being sarcastic about him. She respected him as a father—and would betray him as a husband. Strange indeed is the human heart, especially a woman's.

Vera's husband, Semyon Vasilevich G——, is distantly related to Princess Ligovsky, and is quartered close to her here. Vera, therefore, is often at the princess's house. I gave my word that I would seek acquaintance with the

Ligovskys and make love to Princess Mary, since that would divert attention from Vera. This will not disturb my plans in the least, and I shall enjoy myself hugely.

Happiness? I have got beyond the stage in which a man seeks nothing but happiness, the period when he wants to fall in love violently and passionately. Now I only want to be loved, and that by very few women. Sometimes (terrible thought!) I feel as if a lasting tie would satisfy me.

There is one thing which I have always considered strange in my make-up. I have never become the slave of a woman that I love, but have, without effort, invariably gained absolute power over her will and her heart. How can this be explained? Perhaps it was because I took love rather lightly, and any woman I had a liaison with was afraid lest I should slip through her fingers. Another possibility is that I was exerting the magnetic influence of a strong organism. Or I may never have happened upon a woman as headstrong as myself.

Let me admit that I don't like determined women. A firm character is unsuitable to a woman.

I can recall, however, having once (only once) met a woman with whom I fell in love though she was so strong-willed that she was not malleable like all my other flames. We parted enemies; yet perhaps had we met five years later, things might have turned out differently.

Vera is ill, very ill, though she will not admit it. I fear that she may be in a decline, or suffering from what the French call *fièvre lente* and the English 'hectic fever' or 'low fever'—there is no equivalent Russian term.

The thunderstorm burst while we were in the grotto, and kept us there for half an hour. She did not make me swear to be true to her, nor ask me whether I had been in love with any other woman since we parted. She trusted me again with her former unconcern. Nor is she mistaken. I shall not be unfaithful to her. She is the only woman in the world whom I would never deceive. I know that we shall soon part anew, perhaps for ever. We shall tread different ways to the tomb. But the memory of her will persist unchanged. I have always assured her of this, and she believes me though she says she doesn't.

At last we said goodbye. She went out, and I followed her with my eyes until her hat was hidden behind bushes and rocks. My heart beat violently, just as after our first parting. How delighted I was at the sensation! It meant that youth and its health-giving storms had come back to me. Or was this only a farewell glance, a last gift, a memory? I venture to think that I still look almost like a boy. Though my face is pale, the complexion remains fresh; my limbs are strong and supple; my hair is thick and curly, my eyes sparkle, and my blood is hot.

As soon as I got home, having had my horse saddled, I mounted, and cantered off into the steppe. I love riding a spirited beast through long grass against the wind that whistles across the wild. Eagerly I inhale the fragrant air with my eyes fixed on the blue distance as I try to make out the misty outlines when they begin to take shape as minute by minute I draw nearer. I may start on my ride with a sad heart and an uneasy mind, but these troubles swiftly vanish. I feel relieved as soon as physical fatigue conquers the heaviness of spirit. There is no woman's glance which I cannot forget when I see the brushwood on the mountains lit up by the southern sun—when I see the blue heavens above me or listen to the sound of a torrent roaring in its rocky bed.

I think that when the Cossacks, yawning in their watch-towers, see me galloping without any obvious reason, they must be puzzled, since as far as dress goes I might be a Circassian. Indeed I have been told that when I am riding in my Circassian kit I look more like a Kabardian than many Kabardians do themselves. In all that concerns my military attire I am most fastidious. There must not be one galloon too many; expensive weapons in a plain setting; the fur on my cap of exactly the right length; boots and gaiters must fit perfectly; inner tunic white, outer tunic dark brown. I have carefully studied the riding of these mountaineers, and nothing can tickle my vanity more than to be told that my seat resembles that of a native of the Caucasus. I keep four horses: one for my own use; three for my friends that they may not be bored by having to ride alone. They delight in making use of my stud, but never come out riding with me.

It was already six o'clock this evening before I realized that dinner-time had arrived, and that my mount was tired. I got to the road which leads from Pyatigorsk to the German settlement, whither visitors at the spa often go for a picnic. This road winds among bushes and dips into gorges along which noisy streams flow between banks decked with grass. Around is an amphitheatre of huge blue mountains: Beshtu, and the peaks known as Mount Snake, Iron Mountain, and the Bald Mountain. At the bottom of one of the gorges I halted to let my horse have a drink.

PRINCESS MARY

While thus engaged, I saw coming along the road a noisy and gaily clad cavalcade. The ladies wore black or dark-blue habits for riding side-saddle; the men were in costumes half-way between those of Circassia and Nijni-Novgorod. Grushnitsky was leading the way with Princess Mary beside him.

Ladies at the spa are still timid about the possibility of Circassian raids in broad daylight. That was why Grushnitsky had a sword and a pair of pistols conspicuously displayed over his ranker's cloak. This heroic rig-out made him look rather absurd. A tall bush hid me from the party, but between the leaves I saw them all plainly enough, and there were signs that the leading pair were having a sentimental conversation. As they came down the slope and Grushnitsky took the bridle of the young lady's horse, I could hear what they were saying. Princess Mary asked:

'Are you going to spend the rest of your life in the Caucasus?'

'What do I care about Russia?' replied her cavalier. 'It is a country where thousands of people will despise me because they are richer than I am, whereas here this coarse cloak that I wear has not deprived me of the favour of your acquaintance.'

PRINCESS MARY

'On the contrary,' said the princess, blushing. Grushnitsky's expression showed his delight.

'My life here,' he went on, 'where I am exposed to the bullets of the tribesmen, is turbulent and swift; but if each year God would vouchsafe me one bright glance from a woman's eyes like that which . . .'

At this point they were so near to me that I thought it expedient to disclose myself. Giving my horse a touch with the whip, I sprang out from behind the bush.

'Good God, a Circassian,' screamed Princess Mary, much alarmed.

Wishing to reassure her, I replied in French, bowing slightly.

'Fear nothing, Princess; I am no more dangerous than your companion.'

She was nonplussed, either owing to the blunder she had made or else because she thought my remark offensive. I hoped that the latter was the true explanation. Grushnitsky favoured me with an angry look.

Late that evening, towards eleven, I was walking under the limes on the boulevard. The town was asleep, for there were very few windows still alight. In three directions I could see black, rocky crests, offshoots of Mashuk, which was overhung by a formidable cloud. Eastward the moon, now on the wane, was rising, and its beams tinged the snowy peaks with silver. The calls of the sentries interrupted the murmur of the hot springs which ran freely all night. Now and again I could hear the clatter of a horse's hoofs in the streets, or the creak of a cart and the melancholy voices of the Tartars. I sat down on a bench to think things over, and urgently desired to liberate my mind by friendly conversation—but with whom? What was Vera doing, I wondered? How much I longed, at that moment, to be pressing her hand.

Suddenly I heard hurried and uneven footsteps. 'Grushnitsky,' I thought. Yes, it was he.

'Where have you been?' I asked.

'At Princess Ligovsky's,' he said, with an air of importance. 'Listening to Mary. She sings so beautifully.'

'There's something you ought to bear in mind,' I put in. 'I bet she doesn't know you're a cadet, for she probably believes you have been degraded to the ranks.'

'Likely enough,' he replied, absently. 'But, after all, that's no concern of mine.'

'Well, I thought it better to remind you.'

'Do you know that you annoyed her terribly in that gully this evening? She thought you intolerably rude. I found it hard to convince her that you'd been decently brought up and are so used to moving in the best circles that you could not possibly have designed to insult her. She says you have a saucy look and much too high an opinion of yourself.'

'I agree with her. But don't you want to defend her?'

'Unfortunately I am not yet entitled to do so.'

'Aha,' I thought. 'That means he hopes to acquire the right.'

'It's all the worse for you,' he continued. 'You will find it hard, now, to get on visiting terms, and that's a pity, for theirs is one of the pleasantest houses I know.'

I could not but smile, inwardly at least.

'I find my own house more agreeable than any other,' I said yawning, as I got up to depart.

'At least you will admit that you behaved badly?' asked Grushnitsky.

'What nonsense! If I feel inclined, I shall go to the Ligovskys' tomorrow evening.'

'Time will show,' he replied.

'Then, to please you, I shall begin to make love to Princess Mary.'

'You will not be able to do that unless she lets you speak to her.'

'I shall only have to wait till your conversation bores her. Good night.'

'I'm inclined for a stroll,' he said. 'I don't feel as if I could sleep yet. Or listen, let's go to the restaurant and gamble. I want to have my senses stirred somehow.'

'I hope you'll lose heavily,' I answered, and went home.

May 28th. Nearly a fortnight has gone by since the last entry, and I have not yet made acquaintance with the Ligovskys. I am awaiting a favourable opportunity. Grushnitsky follows Princess Mary like a shadow, and their talks go on without end. I wonder when she will begin to get bored. Her mother is not worrying because Grushnitsky pays attentions to Mary, since she does not regard him as a possible husband for her daughter. The logic is defective. I have twice or thrice noticed the exchange of tender glances between the young people, and it is expedient I should put a stop to this.

Yesterday Vera came to the spring for the first time. Since we met at the grotto she has not left her rooms. At the same moment we emptied our glasses, and, leaning towards me, she whispered:

'You had better make the Ligovskys' acquaintances. Theirs is the only house where we can meet.'

PRINCESS MARY

The implied reproach is tiresome, but I have earned it.

Luckily there is to be a subscription dance tomorrow in the restaurant. I intend to have Princess Mary as my partner for the mazurka.

May 29th. The great dining-hall was transformed into a ballroom. By nine everyone was there. Princess Ligovsky and her daughter were among the last arrivals, and many of the ladies looked jealous because Mary was so tastefully dressed. But those who considered themselves the local aristocracy swallowed their feelings, and went up to greet the pair. What else could they do? Wherever women meet in society, you will always find that upper and lower circles begin to form.

Among a crowd outside the window Grushnitsky was standing, his face close to the opening and his eyes fixed upon his goddess, who nodded slightly every time she passed. He beamed like the sun. The dancing began with a polonaise; then the band played a waltz, so that the men's spurs clinked and their coat-tails flew.

I was standing behind a stout woman who was richly decked with heavy pink plumes. The fantastic splendour of her dress recalled the days of hooped petticoats; and the roughness of her mottled skin reminded me, somehow, of the happy epoch of black patches. A very large wart on her neck was hidden as much as possible by the clasp of her necklace. To her partner, a captain of dragoons, she said:

'Young Princess Ligovsky is an insufferable girl. Can you believe it? She jostled me and never apologized, but merely turned and stared at me through her lorgnette. One can't put up with that sort of thing. She's frightfully arrogant, and ought to be taught a lesson.'

'Not much difficulty about that,' said the dragoon, making for the next room.

Immediately I went up to Princess Mary and asked her for the next waltz, since the free-and-easy conventions of the spa made it possible to dance with a lady to whom one had not been introduced.

She found it hard to restrain a triumphant smile, but managed in the end to assume an indifferent and even distant expression. Dropping her hand lightly on my shoulder, she held her head a little on one side and we started. Never had I put my arm round a more charming and supple figure. I felt her breath on my face; while now and again, in the whirl of the waltz, a lock of her hair detached itself from the others and touched my hot cheek. We went round the room thrice. I found her a magnificent dancer. She was a little out of breath and her eyes looked troubled when we stopped. Through her half-shut lips she could scarcely utter the customary 'Thank you, Sir.'

After a brief silence I said, with the utmost humility:

'I have been told, Princess, that I was unlucky enough to earn your displeasure, though at the time I had not the honour of your acquaintance. You considered me rude, I heard. Can this be true?'

'Is it your aim, now, to confirm me in my opinion?' she asked with a quizzical smile—an expression well suited to her mobile countenance.

'If I actually was so rude as to offend you in some way, permit me the even greater liberty of asking your forgiveness. Indeed, I should value the chance of proving that your opinion was unjustified.'

'To give you that chance would be rather difficult.'

'Why?'

'Because you don't come to our house; and these subscription dances, probably, are rather infrequent.'

'That means,' I thought, 'that your doors are closed as far as I am concerned.'

Being a little peeved, I said: 'You know, Princess, it is not fair to turn your back on a repentant sinner. That may make him twice as bad as before; and then....'

Laughing and whispering among the bystanders came to my ears, and made me break off. A few steps from us was a group of men, among whom was the captain of dragoons I had heard say it would be easy to teach young Princess Ligovsky a lesson. He seemed very much pleased about something, gesticulated, spoke in undertones to his friends. Suddenly a civilian in evening dress, a man with a long moustache and a red face, detached himself from the crowd, and walked unsteadily towards the princess. He was obviously drunk. Halting in front of the embarrassed Mary, he put his hands behind his back, stared at her fixedly with his grey eyes, and said in a hoarse falsetto:

'Excuse me. What was I going to say? Oh, I remember. Will you dance the mazurka with me?'

'What do you want?' she said, her voice trembling as she looked round with agitation and alarm. No help offered. Her mother was far away, and none of the men in the neighbour-

PRINCESS MARY

ing group were among her acquaintances. Probably one of the aides-de-camp could see what was going on, but he kept his distance behind the crowd, not wishing to be mixed up in the affair.

'Well,' said the drunken man, winking at the captain of dragoons, who was urging him by signs. 'Do you really not want to dance with me? Once more I have the honour of requesting you to be my partner in the mazurka. Perhaps you think me drunk? What does it matter if I am? Let me assure you that I shall dance all the better for being a little screwed.'

I saw that she was nearly fainting from fear and indignation, so I went up to the drunken man, took a firm grip of his arm, looked him steadily in the eyes, and asked him to go away, saying: 'Princess Ligovsky has for some time been engaged to me for that dance.'

'All right. Another time, then,' he said with a laugh, and rejoined his friends who, somewhat ashamed, promptly took him into another room.

I was rewarded by a grateful glance from Princess Mary, who then went to her mother and explained what had happened. The latter sought me out and thanked me. Princess Ligovsky said she had known my mother, and that several of my aunts had been her friends.

'I can't think why you and I have not got to know one another before,' she added. 'But I suppose you will admit that you chiefly are to blame. The way in which you shun society is unparalleled. I hope the atmosphere of my drawing-room will make you less splenetic.'

I produced a phrase appropriate to the occasion.

The quadrilles went on for ages. At last came the turn of the mazurka, and I sat it out with Princess Mary.

I said nothing about the drunken man, nor about my behaviour in the gulch, nor about Grushnitsky. The impression which the disagreeable scene in the ballroom had made on her was gradually expunged. Her face cleared, and we laughed pleasantly as we talked. Her conversation was shrewd, unaffected, lively, and easy, sometimes even profound. In rather tangled phrases I gave her to understand that I had liked her for a long time. Inclining her head in acknowledgment, she blushed slightly.

'You're a strange man,' she then said, raising her velvet eyes and smiling with some embarrassment.

'I had a sufficient reason for not seeking to make your acquaintance. You have so many

PRINCESS MARY

admirers that I was afraid of getting lost in the crowd.'

'You need not have been afraid. They're a tedious lot.'

'All of them? Without exception?'

She looked at me earnestly, as if trying to recall something. Then, with another blush, she said:

'All of them, without exception.'

'Even my friend Grushnitsky? Is he a bore too?'

'So that gentleman is your friend?' she asked, dubiously.

'Yes.'

'Well, in that case, I suppose he cannot be accounted a bore.'

'He comes into the category of unfortunates, then?' I said, with a laugh.

'Of course. But do you consider that funny? I should like to see you in his shoes.'

'What if I were? I was a cadet myself, once; and it was the happiest time of my life.'

'Is he really a cadet?' she said quickly. Then she added: 'But I thought . . .'

'What did you think?'

'Nothing. Who is that lady?'

The conversation took another turn, and we did not say any more about Grushnitsky.

The mazurka came to an end, and we said:

PRINCESS MARY

'Goodbye till we meet again.' The ladies left the ballroom; I went to get some supper, and met Werner.

'Hullo!' he said to me. 'You're not to be depended on. You said you only wanted to make the young lady's acquaintance by saving her from the jaws of death.'

'I've done better than that,' I answered. 'I saved her from fainting at the ball.'

'How? Please explain.'

'Damned if I do. Find out for yourself, since you are such an expert at solving riddles.'

May 30th. At about seven in the evening I went for a stroll on the boulevard. Grushnitsky, having caught sight of me from a distance, came up. His eyes were shining with a somewhat ludicrous ecstasy. Shaking my hand cordially, he said in a tragical tone:

'Thanks so much, Pechorin. Do you understand why I am grateful?'

'No, I can't say I do, for you've really nothing to thank me for,' I answered, being quite unaware of having done him a good turn.

'What about yesterday? You can't possibly have forgotten. Mary told me all about it.'

'Do you share everything with her, even gratitude?'

PRINCESS MARY

'Look here,' rejoined Grushnitsky, pompously, 'if you wish to keep on friendly terms with me, you mustn't be jocose about my love. I am madly in love with her, and I think—I hope—that my love is returned. I have a favour to ask. You are going to the Ligovskys' this evening, aren't you? Take careful note of everything that happens. You have experience in these matters, and know more about women than I do. Women, women, who can understand them? Their smiles give the lie to their looks; their words promise and beckon, while the tone of their voice repels. At one moment they plumb the depths of a man's mind, and at the next they fail to understand his plainest utterance. Consider this young princess. Yesterday her eyes burned with passion whenever she looked at me; today they are lustreless and cold.'

'Perhaps the change is the effect of the waters,' I put in.

'You always look at things so prosaically, materialist that you are,' he said disdainfully. 'If we are to be materialists, we will discuss matters of a material kind.'

His bad pun, utterly childish though it was, cheered him up.

At nine we went to the princess's together.

As we passed Vera's window I caught sight

PRINCESS MARY

of her, and we exchanged glances. She came into the drawing-room very soon, and Princess Ligovsky introduced her as a relative.

Tea was served. There were many guests, and we joined in a general conversation. Wishing to please our hostess, I was humorous, told some quaint anecdotes, and made her laugh several times. Princess Mary, I could see, would also have liked to laugh, but restrained the impulse, since merriment would have been out of keeping with the role she wished to play. She wanted to appear languid, and this was not a bad choice. Grushnitsky was indubitably pleased that she did not succumb to my mood.

When we had had tea, we went into the hall.

'I hope you are pleased that I have obeyed you,' I said in an undertone to Vera, as I passed her.

She looked at me both affectionately and gratefully. I had got accustomed to these glances in course of time, but they used to make me feel rapturous.

The young princess sat down at the piano, since there was a widely expressed desire for her to sing. Holding my peace, and taking advantage of the hubbub, I went to the window with Vera, who said she had something to tell

PRINCESS MARY

me, a matter of urgency to us both. It proved to be of no consequence whatever.

Meanwhile Princess Mary was feeling vexed by my indifference, as she showed me by the flash of anger in her eyes. How well I understand this silent language, which is expressive and vigorous, though tacit.

She had a good voice, but it was untrained, so I did not care to attend. Grushnitsky, as he leaned on the piano facing her, devoured her with his eyes, and kept on murmuring: 'Charming, delicious.'

'Listen to me,' said Vera. 'I would rather you did not get to know my husband; but you really must make yourself agreeable to Princess Ligovsky. That will come easily to you, as does everything which you really want. This is the only place where we can meet.'

'The only place?'

Blushing, she went on: 'You know that I am your slave, and that I have never been able to disregard your wishes. I shall be punished for it, now that you have ceased to love me. But at least my reputation must be kept unspotted— not for my own sake, as you know perfectly well. But I entreat you not to torture me by needless doubts and assumed coldness. I shall probably die very soon, for I feel that my strength is ebbing day by day. All the same, I don't bother to think about a future life, for my thoughts are wholly devoted to you. You men simply don't understand the joy of a fleeting glance, of a pressure of the hand. I swear to you, however, that the mere sound of your voice gives me a more intense joy than I feel in the most passionate of kisses.'

Now the young princess had finished singing. There was a general murmur of applause. I went up to her when the others had paid their tribute, and said something rather commonplace about her voice.

Pouting a little, she curtsied in derision.

'I am flattered all the more because you were not listening. I suppose you don't care for music?'

'On the contrary, I am very fond of it, especially after dinner.'

'Grushnitsky was right when he declared that you have an extremely prosaic mind. I see that you only like music for gastronomic reasons.'

'Wrong again! I am not a gourmet, but I have a rather poor digestion. Music after my midday meal has a sedative effect, and a doze at that hour does me good, so I like music for medical reasons. But in the evening it agitates my nerves, making me too gloomy or too cheerful. Either is a nuisance, when there is no adequate cause for sorrow or for joy. Besides, to pull a long face in society makes one look ridiculous, and excessively good spirits are equally inappropriate.'

Losing interest in my words, she left me, and sat down beside Grushnitsky. They began some sort of sentimental conversation. Though she tried to pretend that she was listening to him attentively, I think she must have answered his stilted phrases absently and beside the point, for now and again he looked at her with surprise, trying to discover what could account for the agitation betrayed by her restless glances.

But I can see through you, my dear little princess. You want to pay me in my own coin, to burst the bubble of my self-esteem. You won't succeed, and if you declare war I shall be ruthless.

In the course of the evening I tried several times to break into their conversation, but she received what I said rather nonchalantly, until at length I departed, feigning annoyance. Mary triumphed, and so did Grushnitsky. Triumph if you like, my friend, but you'd better be quick, for you won't have much time to enjoy yourselves. How can you? I have a presentiment. As soon as I get to know a woman, I can infallibly discern whether she will fall in love with me or not.

I spent the rest of the evening with Vera, talking intermittently about old times. Why does she love me so much? Hard to explain, especially seeing that she is the only woman who has thoroughly understood me—weaknesses, evil passions, and all. Is evil really so attractive?

Grushnitsky and I left together. As soon as we were in the street, he took my arm, and, after a long silence, said:

'Well, what do you think of her?'

'You poor boob,' I should have liked to answer, but held my tongue, and was content to shrug my shoulders.

June 6th. During all these days I have stuck to the same system. The young princess is beginning to enjoy my conversation. I have been telling her some of my strange adventures, and she thinks me a remarkable man. To her I make fun of everything in the world, and especially of the feelings. This is frightening her, rather. When I am present, she does not venture to have sentimental arguments with Grushnitsky, and more than once I've heard her answer one of his tirades with a scornful smile. Whenever he goes up to her, I put on a resigned expression, and

PRINCESS MARY

leave them to themselves. The first time I did this, she was glad, or feigned to be. The second time she was angry with me. The third time—with Grushnitsky.

'You have very little vanity,' she said to me yesterday. 'Why do you think I like being with Grushnitsky?'

I replied that I was sacrificing my own pleasure to my friend's happiness.

'My pleasure too,' she said.

I looked at her steadily and assumed a grave expression. After that I did not say a word to her for the rest of the day. In the evening she was silent, and this morning at the spring even more so. When I approached her, she was listening absently to Grushnitsky, who (it seemed) was in raptures about the beauties of nature. As soon as she caught sight of me, she began to laugh—quite in the wrong place, making as if she did not see me. I drew to a corner whence I could watch her unseen. Turning away from her companion, she yawned twice. Certainly Grushnitsky has become a bore to her.

I won't say a word to her for another two days.

June 11th. I often ask myself why I take so much trouble to win the love of a young girl whom I have no wish to seduce and whom I shall never make my wife. For what purpose this feminine coquetry on my part? Vera is more deeply in love with me than Princess Mary ever will be with anyone. Nor does she even seem to me one of the invincible, unapproachable beauties. Were she that, the difficulty of the enterprise might prove a lure.

Nothing of the sort here. Consequently there is no question of the restless need for love that torments us in youth, hurries us from one woman to another, until we find a woman who can't endure us. Then begins our phase of constancy, a genuine unending passion, mathematically representable as a line proceeding from a point into space. The secret of this endlessness is that it has become simply impossible to reach one's aim or end.

Why then do I take so much trouble? Am I jealous of Grushnitsky? Poor fellow, he is certainly not worthy of that. Or is it the outcome of the malicious, irresistible feeling which impels us to destroy a neighbour's most valued illusions, that we may have the cheap pleasure of saying to him, when he comes to us in despair and begs to be told what remains for him to trust:

'Friend, just the same thing once happened

to me, but you can see that now I dine, sup, and sleep as if there were nothing amiss, and I hope I am ready to face death without howling or sobbing.'

Yet there is ecstasy in mastering a young heart that is like a flower which has scarcely begun to unfold its petals, or like a flower which exhales its sweetest scent when it is first touched by the rays of the rising sun. Pluck it at that instant, inhale the perfume, and then throw it on the roadside. Someone may pick it up. I have an insatiable eagerness to grasp everything that I meet on my way through life. I see the sufferings and the joys of others only in relation to myself, I regard them as food to nourish my spiritual strength. It has become impossible for me to do foolish deeds under the stimulus of passion. In me ambition has been crushed by circumstances, to assume another form. For ambition is nothing more than the thirst for power, and my chief delight is to impose my will upon all with whom I come in contact. To inspire in others a feeling of love, devotion, or fear, what is it but the first sign and the greatest triumph of power? To be for someone a cause of suffering or joy, without the least right—can pride know sweeter food than this?

What, indeed, is happiness? Gratified pride.

PRINCESS MARY

If I regarded myself as the best and most powerful person in the world, I should be perfectly happy; or if everyone loved me, and I could consider myself a perpetual source of love. Evil begets evil. Suffering is the first experience that enables us to take delight in tormenting others. The idea of evil cannot enter a man's head without arousing the desire for its practical realization. Ideas, it has been said, are organic creations. Birth gives them form, and this form is action. The man in whose head the most numerous ideas have been born, acts most powerfully on others. That is why a genius who is made fast to a desk in an office will die or go mad; just as a man with a vigorous constitution who is compelled to lead a sedentary life and whose activities are restricted will die of an apoplectic stroke.

Passions are nothing but ideas newly born; they belong to the youth of the heart, and only a fool believes that they will go on troubling him till the end of a long life. Many tranquil rivers begin as noisy torrents, nor is there any river which rushes and foams throughout its whole course to the sea. Tranquillity in a man is often a sign of great though hidden strength, for fullness and depth of feelings and thoughts are incompatible with wild outbursts. The soul,

PRINCESS MARY

in suffering and in joy, keeps strict account of itself, and knows that this is needful. It is sure that, if there is no rain, the continuous heat of the sun will wither it. It is permeated with its own life, it caresses and punishes itself as if it were a beloved child. Only when he reaches this high state of self-knowledge can a man understand the meaning of God's justice.

As I read over what I have been writing, I become aware that I have strayed a long way from my subject. What does that matter? I am writing this diary for myself, and whatever I put into it will, with the lapse of time, become a cherished memory.

Grushnitsky came to my rooms and flung his arms round my neck—he had just received his commission. We drank champagne to celebrate the event. Then Werner turned up.

'I'm sorry I can't congratulate you, old man,' he said, when informed of what had happened.

'Why on earth not?'

'Because that ranker's cloak you are wearing suits you very well, but I fancy that an infantry officer's uniform made by a local tailor will transform you into a far less interesting figure. Hitherto you've been an exception, but henceforward you'll be commonplace.'

'I don't care what you say, Doctor; you won't spoil my pleasure,' rejoined Grushnitsky. Then he whispered to me: 'Werner doesn't know what hopes my epaulets will give me. O epaulets, O epaulets, your stars are guiding stars. That's why I bubble over with happiness.'

'Are you coming with me to the crater?' I asked.

'No, I don't want the princess to see me till my uniform is ready.'

'Shall I tell her the good news?'

'Not a word, please. I want it to come as a surprise.'

'Tell me one thing. How does your courtship advance?'

He was silent from embarrassment, for he would have been glad to answer me with a braggart's lie, and yet he was ashamed, while he was equally ashamed of acknowledging the truth.

'Do you think she's in love with you?' I asked.

'In love with me? I say, Pechorin, you have some queer notions. How could she be, so soon? Even if she were, no decent woman would acknowledge it.'

'Good. I suppose, too, that according to you no decent man would have declared his passion so soon?'

'Oh, well, my dear fellow, there are ways, and

ways. Love is often disclosed without a word being said about it.'

'True. But the love that is only read in the eyes does not bind a woman as words do. Watch out, Grushnitsky. She is only fooling you.'

'You think she's fooling me?' he rejoined with a self-satisfied smile. 'I'm sorry for you, Pechorin, but you're really rather an ass.'

With that, he departed.

In the evening many people used to walk to a neighbouring hollow, which local geologists regard as the crater of an extinct volcano. It was on the slopes of Mashuk, nearly a mile from the town. A narrow path led thither through bushes and rocks. I went there with Princess Mary and offered her my arm up the hill. She took it gladly, and never let go during the whole of our walk.

Our conversation began in a rather spiteful vein. I talked about our various acquaintances, one by one, dilating first upon their absurdity and then upon their meanness. My gall became intensified, for though I started in jest I finished in deadly earnest. Consequently she passed from amusement to alarm.

'You're a dangerous man,' she said. 'I would rather be stabbed by an assassin's dagger than by your tongue. If you have a taste for speaking evil of me, I beg you to stab me instead. I think you will find that easy enough.'

'You really consider me an assassin?'

'Worse, if possible.'

I thought for a minute, and then said, pretending to be profoundly moved:

'Such has been my fate since early childhood. Everyone has read in my face the signs of bad qualities which were not really there until they were born out of the very supposition. I was shy, but, being accused of craftiness, I became secretive. Though I was profoundly aware of the difference between good and evil, I got no caresses, everybody wounded me, with the result that I became bitter and spiteful. I was sulky when other children were cheerful and responsive. Though I felt superior to them, I was thrust into a lower place. This made me jealous. I was ready to love the whole world, but no one understood me, and I learned to hate. My joyless youth was spent in a struggle with myself and the world. Afraid of ridicule, I hid my finest feelings in the depths of my heart, and there they perished. I spoke the truth, but nobody believed me, so I began to tell lies. Being well acquainted with the world and the motive forces of society, I became an adept in the science of life, but I saw that others were happy though they lacked my skill, and enjoyed their advantages without having (like me) struggled hard to obtain them. Despair mastered me—not despair of the kind which can only be cured by a pistol-shot, but a chilly and feeble despair which wears the mask of kindliness and amiability. Substantially, I was a cripple. Half of my mind had ceased to exist, having evaporated and dried up till it perished, so I cut it off, determined to fling it away. But it stirred once more, to live for the service of all. No one noticed this, for no one was aware of the existence of the decayed half of me. You have revived the memory of it, and I have read you its epitaph. In the general view, epitaphs are ridiculous. I don't agree, especially when I recall what lies beneath them. However, I don't ask you to share my opinion, and if my outburst merely amuses you, please laugh. Let me assure you that I shall not mind in the least.'

At this moment I met her eyes, and saw that there were tears in them. Her hand trembled on my arm, her cheeks flamed. She was sorry for me. Sympathy, an emotion to which women are prone, had thrust its claws into her inexperienced heart. Throughout the walk she had been absent-minded, and showed no inclination to look flirtatiously at anyone—notable signs.

We reached the crater. The other ladies

separated from their escorts, but she continued to hold my arm. The men's jests did not amuse her, nor was she alarmed by the steepness of the slope on which she was standing, though the rest of the women screamed and shut their eyes.

On the way home I did not continue our touching conversation, but asked pointless questions and made jokes to which she replied briefly and inattentively.

'Have you ever been in love?' I asked at length.

She looked fixedly at me, shook her head, and then relapsed into a brown study. Obviously she wanted to say something, but did not know how to begin. Her bosom heaved. What was she to do? A muslin sleeve is a poor defence, and an electric current passed from my arm to her hand. Passion nearly always begins in this way, and we are apt to deceive ourselves by thinking that a woman loves us for our physical or moral merits. Of course these may prepare the way, may predispose her heart for the sacred fire; but it is the first touch which decides matters.

'I've been really nice to you today, haven't I?' asked Princess Mary, with an embarrassed smile, when we got back from our walk.

We said goodbye.

She is dissatisfied with herself, and thinks she

has been too cold. This is the first, the most important advance. Tomorrow she will want to reward me. I know it all by heart. That is why I find it such a bore.

June 12th. I saw Vera today. She annoyed me by her jealousy. Princess Mary, I gathered, had been seized by the fancy of revealing all the secrets of her heart. An undesirable confidant, it must be admitted.

'I can see how things are pointing,' said Vera. 'You'd better tell me plainly right away that you love her.'

'What if I don't?'

'Then why do you pester her, disturb her, trouble her imagination? I know you through and through. If you want me to believe you, come this week to Kislovodsk. My husband and I are going there the day after tomorrow. Princess Ligovsky will stay here a little longer. Take rooms next door to us. We shall be quartered on the mezzanine of a large house close to the spring. When the Ligovskys come they will be on the floor below ours. The house next door, which belongs to the same landlord, is still unlet. Will you come?'

I promised, and that very day I sent over to engage the rooms.

Grushnitsky came to see me at six, and said that tomorrow he would get his uniform, just in time for the ball.

'At last I shall be able to dance the whole evening with Mary. We shall have such a talk.'

'When is the ball?'

'Tomorrow, I tell you. But didn't you know? There's to be a big fête, which the local authorities are organizing.'

'Shall we go for a walk now on the boulevard, before supper?'

'Not for anything, in this horrid cloak.'

'A new tune. I thought you were in love with it.'

So I went for my stroll unaccompanied, and, meeting Princess Mary, asked her if she'd dance the mazurka with me next day. She was both surprised and pleased.

'I thought you only danced when you had to, like last time,' she said, with a charming smile.

Apparently she had never noticed Grushnitsky's absence.

'You will have an agreeable surprise tomorrow,' I said.

'What's that?'

'A great secret. But you'll discover it yourself at the ball.'

PRINCESS MARY

I spent the rest of the evening at the Ligovskys'. There was nobody else there except Vera, and a queer old codger. Being in the vein, I improvised some adventure stories. The young princess was sitting opposite to me, and listened to my nonsense with such profound, eager, almost affectionate attention, that I felt ashamed I was romancing. What had become now of her liveliness, her coquetry, her caprices, her disdainful mien, her contemptuous smile, and her pretence of aloofness?

Vera noticed everything. There was a look of profound melancholy on her face, which was ravaged by illness. She was in a deep armchair, near the window and dimly lit. I felt sorry for her.

Then I told the whole story of my acquaintance with her, and of our love—of course using assumed names for the hero and heroine.

So realistically did I describe my tender feeling for her, my anxiety, and my joy, while setting her conduct and her character in the most favourable light, that she could not help forgiving me my flirtation with the princess.

Rising from the armchair, she came over and sat down close to us. Now she grew more animated, and we kept it up till two in the morning before she remembered that by doctor's orders she ought to have been in bed three hours ago.

June 13*th.* Half an hour before the ball, Grushnitsky arrived at my rooms in the full splendour of an infantry officer's uniform. To his third button was attached a bronze chain from which hung a double lorgnette. His epaulets, of preposterous size, turned upwards at the outer ends, so that they looked like Cupid's wings. His boots squeaked. In his left hand he held a pair of brown kid gloves and his cap, while with his right he was persistently twisting a tuft of hair into little curls. The look on his face was a queer mixture of self-approval and lack of confidence. His overdressed appearance and arrogant bearing aroused in me a strong desire to laugh, but such a manifestation would not have squared with my plans.

Flinging his cap and gloves on the table, he began to pull down his coat-tails and titivate himself before the mirror. An enormous black kerchief twisted round the high collar which supported his chin projected about an inch. Thinking this too little, he pulled it up till it reached his ears. He found the adjustment hard work, for the collar of the uniform was tight and

PRINCESS MARY

uncomfortable, and the effort gave his face a strong flush.

'They say that you're making violent love to my princess,' he said carelessly, without glancing at me.

'They say! What do they say? Let them say!' I answered, to show that this must be idle talk which went for nothing.

'Look here,' Grushnitsky continued, 'does my uniform really fit? That wretched Jew of a tailor has made a tunic which cuts me under the arms. Have you any scent?'

'Surely you don't need any more scent? You positively stink of attar of roses.'

'Never mind. I know what I want. Hand over the bottle.'

I did so, and he half emptied it upon his tie, his handkerchief, and his sleeves.

'Are you going to dance?' he asked.

'I don't think so.'

'I'm afraid the princess and I will have to begin the mazurka, and I hardly know as much as one of the figures.'

'Have you asked her to dance the mazurka with you?'

'No, not yet, but . . .'

'Take care. Someone else may have been beforehand.'

'What rot,' he answered. 'Goodbye. I shall wait for her at the entrance.'

Picking up his cap, he hurried off.

I started in half an hour. The street was dark and empty, but round the club or restaurant (whichever you like to call it) was a large crowd. The windows were lighted up, and the sounds of a regimental band came to my ears down the evening breeze. I walked slowly, for I felt depressed. 'Is it possible,' I thought, 'that I have nothing on earth to do but frustrate others' hopes.' From the time since I first became active in life fate has continually involved me in the unravelling of other peoples' dramas, as if it were impossible for them either to die or to sink into despair unless I were on hand. I have always been needed on the stage in the last act, involuntarily assuming the disagreeable role of executioner or traitor. What has been destiny's purpose in this? I do hope I was not foreordained to be the author of middle-class tragedies and family romances or to become a collaborator in filling the shelves of circulating libraries. I really don't know. Many begin life with the idea of becoming an Alexander the Great or a Lord Byron, yet never achieve anything more magnificent than the position of a subordinate civil servant.

PRINCESS MARY

Entering the ballroom, I mingled with the throng of men and began to watch what was going on. Grushnitsky was standing next to the princess and talking volubly with excitement. She listened idly, looking all round as she held her fan to her lips. Her expression was petulant, and her eyes were obviously in search of someone. Drawing near behind them, as quietly as I could, I listened to what they were saying.

'You are tormenting me, Princess,' interjected Grushnitsky. 'There has been a terrible change since I last saw you.'

'You have changed also,' she replied, glancing at him, her look being charged with hidden scorn which he failed to detect.

'I have changed, you think? No, that's impossible. Whoever has once seen you will for ever carry with him your divine image.'

'Oh, dry up,' she said sarcastically.

'Why is it that you grow impatient when I repeat something you have so often heard me say, and which used to please you?'

'Repetition palls on me at last.'

'What a bitter disappointment. I thought—fool that I was—these epaulets, at least, would give me the right to hope. I see that I should have done better to go on wearing my ranker's cloak, to which, perhaps, I owed the honour of your attention.'

'Well, I certainly think you looked much nicer in your cloak.'

At this point I thought fit to show myself and bow to the princess. Blushing a little, she said:

'Don't you agree, Monsieur Pechorin, that Monsieur Grushnitsky's grey cloak suited him much better?'

'I don't quite agree,' I answered. 'In officer's uniform he looks even more boyish.'

To Grushnitsky this came as a blow. Like adolescents in general, he likes to pretend that he is a full-grown man, believing the marks of youth on his face to be the signs of maturity. Looking at me furiously, he stamped, and left us alone together.

'You must admit,' I said to the princess, 'that though he's always been a laughable figure, a little while ago he seemed interesting to you—in his grey cloak.'

Lowering her eyes, she left my remark unanswered.

Throughout the evening Grushnitsky continued to pester Mary for dances, devouring her with his eyes, sighing, wearying her with entreaties and reproaches. By the time the

PRINCESS MARY

third quadrille came, she was heartily sick of him.

'I never expected this of you,' he said, coming up to me and taking me by the arm.

'Didn't expect what?'

'Aren't you going to dance the mazurka with her?' he asked portentously. 'That's what she's told me.'

'What on earth are you talking about? It's not been a secret, has it?'

'Obviously. It's just what I might have expected from a girl, from a flirt. But I shall have my revenge.'

'You can blame your cloak or your epaulets, as you please, but why should you blame her? You have no right to do that because she doesn't like you any more.'

'For what reason did she give me hopes?'

'For what reason did you hope? I can understand wanting a thing, and fighting for it; but hope is no good.'

The mazurka began. Grushnitsky chose no one but the princess as his partner, and other men did the same; it was manifestly a plot against me. So much the better. If she wants to talk to me and they prevent her, she will want it twice as much.

Twice I pressed her hand. The second time she withdrew it, without saying a word.

'I shall sleep badly tonight,' she said to me when the mazurka was finished.

'That will be Grushnitsky's fault.'

'Oh, no.'

Her face became so thoughtful, so sad, that I determined to give myself the pleasure of kissing her hand before the evening was over.

People began to leave for home. Helping the princess into her carriage, I raised her little hand to my lips. The street was dark, and no one could see me.

I was thoroughly satisfied with myself as I went back into the ballroom.

Some young men, among whom was Grushnitsky, were seated at a large table, having supper. When I went in, the conversation suddenly ceased. It was plain they had been talking about me. Many of them had been annoyed with me since the previous ball, especially the captain of dragoons. Now, it seemed, a definite conspiracy was being organized against me under the leadership of Grushnitsky. He looked proud and valiant.

Well, I'm very glad, for I love enemies—though not precisely in the sense of the Sermon on the Mount. They amuse me, and stir my blood. To be unceasingly on guard to catch the meaning of every glance and every word, to guess intentions and baffle adversaries, to simulate being deceived and then with one push to overturn the whole great edifice which has been built of craft and fraud—that is what I call living.

While supper lasted, Grushnitsky went on whispering to the captain of dragoons and exchanging signs with him.

June 14th. Today Vera and her husband removed to Kislovodsk. I met their carriage when I was on the way to the Ligovskys'. She nodded to me, but her eyes were reproachful.

Yet which of us is to blame? Why won't she give me a chance of seeing her alone? Love is like fire; if not fed with fuel, it dies down. Perhaps jealousy will do what my entreaties have failed to achieve.

I sat at the princess's a whole hour. Mary did not appear, for she was ailing. Nor was she on the boulevard this evening. The newly-hatched conspiracy, equipped with lorgnettes, has assumed a formidable aspect. I was glad that Mary was indisposed, for the young men were quite capable of open rudeness. Grushnitsky's hair was ruffled, and he looked desperate. This time, it appears, he is really hurt, his vanity having been wounded. But there are persons in whom even despair is ludicrous.

On my way home I felt that there had been something wanting. I hadn't seen her, and she was out of sorts. Is it possible that I have fallen in love with her. What nonsense!

June 15th. At eleven in the morning, an hour when Princess Ligovsky is usually sweating in the Ermolovsky bath-house, I passed their quarters. Princess Mary, plunged in thought, was sitting at the window. On catching sight of me, she jumped up.

I entered the hall, but nobody was there, so, taking advantage of the unconventionality of a spa, I went into the drawing-room without being announced.

Mary's pretty face was deathly pale. She was standing close to the piano, with one hand on the back of a chair. This hand was trembling. Going up to her I said:

'Are you angry with me?'

Raising her tired eyes to look at me, she shook her head. Her lips wanted to say something, but couldn't. Tears ran down her cheeks. Sinking into the chair, she covered her face with her hands.

'What is the matter with you?' I asked, taking one of them in mine.

PRINCESS MARY

'You don't respect me. Please leave me.'

I walked a few steps away. She sat up in the chair, her eyes flashing.

Holding the door-handle, I stopped and said:

'Forgive me, Princess. I behaved like a madman. It shan't happen a second time. I shall take measures to stop it. How could you know what has been going on in my mind since then? You never will know, and all the better for you. Goodbye.'

As I went out I fancied I heard her crying.

Till evening I roamed about the slopes of Mashuk, getting very tired, so that when I reached home I flung myself on my bed completely exhausted.

Werner came to see me and said:

'Is it true that you're going to marry the young princess?'

'What are you talking about?'

'The whole town is agog with it. My patients are full of the great news. As is the way of patients, they hear all the gossip.'

'Grushnitsky's at the bottom of this,' I thought. To Werner I said:

'In order to convince you, Doctor, that you've heard a false report, I will tell you a secret. Tomorrow I leave for Kislovodsk.'

PRINCESS MARY

'Princess Mary, too?'

'No, she is going to stay here another week.'

'Then you're not going to marry her?'

'Look at me, Doctor. Have I the appearance of an engaged man, or anything like it?'

'I can't say you have. But you know there are circumstances in which an honourable man may be compelled to marry, whether he wants to or not, and there are mothers who don't try to prevent such circumstances arising. Anyhow as your friend I advise you to be more careful. The atmosphere of these waters is very dangerous. I've seen so many fine young fellows worthy of a better fate who have gone straight away from here to get married. Would you believe it, someone once wanted to marry me? The mother was a provincial, and her daughter was anaemic. I was ill-advised enough to remark that the colour would come back to the girl's face when she married. With tears in her eyes the mother thereupon gratefully offered me the young woman's hand and entire fortune—fifty serfs, I believe. I answered that I was not in a position to marry.'

Werner departed firmly convinced that he had given me fair warning.

Certainly he had made it plain enough that malicious rumours about me and the young princess were rife in the town. Grushnitsky shall pay for this.

June 18*th*. It's three days already since I came to Kislovodsk. I see Vera every morning at the spring or when I go for a walk. As soon as I wake, I sit at the window and look at her veranda through my lorgnette. She is already dressed and awaiting the pre-arranged sign. We meet, as if by chance, in the garden which runs down to the spring from our houses. The life-giving air of the mountains has already restored her colour and strength. Not without good cause do the Circassians speak of the waters of Narsan, the principal fountain of this spa, as 'the drink of heroes'. People who live here declare that the air of Kislovodsk stimulates love, and that the place is the scene of the fulfilment of all the romances which have begun upon the declivities of Mashuk. In fact everything in the neighbourhood breathes solitude. All here is secret and mysterious. We have thick shade in the avenue of the limes whose branches interlace overhead, while below runs a stream which gurgles from rock to rock as it cuts its channel through the green hills. Ravines, full of mist and silence, branch off on both sides. The atmosphere is pervaded by the scent of tall southern grasses and white acacia. Without pause one is lulled by the murmur of the chill rivulets which approach one another as they near the end of the valley, to run amicably side by side until they fall into the Podkumok.

On this shore the ravine expands into a broader hollow, which is traversed by a dusty winding road. It seems to me that every time I glance in that direction there are carriages driving up. But hers has not yet come.

The suburb beyond the fort is thickly peopled. In the restaurant on the hill a few paces from my rooms lights twinkle in the evening through the double row of poplars. Noise and the clink of glasses go on all night. I have never been in a place where people dilute their wine so much with mineral water as here. I agree with Griboedoff that this dilution is a mistake.

Grushnitsky and his pals hold high revel in the restaurant, but they hardly vouchsafe me a greeting when we encounter one another.

The recently commissioned officer did not arrive till yesterday, but already since coming he has picked a quarrel with three old men who claimed priority at the bath. His reverses certainly seem to have made him pugnacious.

June 22nd. At last they've come. I was sitting at

the window when I heard the gride of their carriage wheels, and my heart leapt. What does this mean? Can I be in love? I'm so stupidly made up that it's quite possible.

I lunched with them. Princess Ligovsky looked at me most affectionately, but never left her daughter alone with me (unfortunately). All the same Vera is jealous of Princess Mary. I find that advantageous. What won't a woman do to annoy a rival? I remember how one woman fell in love with me because I loved another. Nothing can be more paradoxical than the feminine mind. How difficult it is to convince a woman of anything. You can only do so when she has convinced herself. The arrangement of the proofs by which they overcome preconceived ideas is most peculiar. If you want to understand their dialectic, you will have to jettison the principles of formal logic. Here is an instance of the accepted method of reasoning.

'This man loves me, but I am married, so I must not love him.'

But a woman reasons thus:

'I must not love this man, for I am married; but he loves me, and so....'

The dots indicate that reason has nothing to say; but the tongue has, the eyes have, and the heart has (if there is one).

PRINCESS MARY

What would happen if someone showed this diary to a woman? She would indignantly protest against being slandered.

Ever since poets have sung and women have read their poems (for which poets are duly grateful), women have been called angels, and in their simplicity, they take compliment for fact—forgetting that poets once idolized Nero, being liberally paid.

Still it is not for me to speak evil of women, for me who find that women are the only things in the world that I love; for me ever ready to sacrifice on behalf of women peace, ambition, my very life. The last thing to suppose is that, vexed and afflicted by injured vanity, I am endeavouring to strip off the veil of magic which only an experienced eye can pierce. No, all that I say of them is the outcome of what Pushkin described in *Eugene Onegin* as, 'The mind's cold observations, and the sorrowful teachings of the heart.'

Women ought to wish that all men should know as much about them as I do, for I love them a hundred times as much as I used to when I was afraid of them and did not understand their little weaknesses.

In passing let me say that Werner recently compared women to the enchanted forest of

PRINCESS MARY

which Tasso speaks in his *Jerusalem Delivered*. 'As soon as you draw near it,' wrote the Italian poet, 'there assail you in all directions such terrors as only God can save you from: duty, pride, conventionality, public opinion, scorn, contempt. You should not look at them, but should go straight on. Little by little the monsters will vanish, and there will open before you a quiet glade in the midst of which a green myrtle blooms. You will have much reason for regret, therefore, if at the first steps you are overwhelmed with misgiving and turn back.'

June 24th. This evening was full of incidents. About two miles from Kislovodsk, in the Podkumok valley, there is a rock known as The Ring, a natural gateway. It is situated on a high hill, and the setting sun shines right through it, like a tongue of flame. A large cavalcade had ridden out to watch this picturesque phenomenon. Truth to tell, however, not one of the party thought much about the sun. I was riding beside the young princess, and on the way home we had to ford the Podkumok. Mountain torrents are always rather dangerous, even when shallow, chiefly because the bed is so changeable. The variations in the current modify it from day to day. Where stones lay yesterday, may twenty-four hours later be a deep hole. Taking the bridle of Mary's horse, I led the beast into the water, which soon reached its knees. We moved gently across the ford, obliquely. When fording these swift streams it is inadvisable to look down at the current, for the sight of it may make the rider giddy. Unfortunately I forgot to warn the princess of this.

About half way over, at a place where the torrent flowed most swiftly, she suddenly swayed in the saddle. 'I don't feel well,' she said in a feeble voice. Leaning towards her, I quickly put my arm round her supple waist.

'Look up, not down,' I said. 'There's no danger. Nothing to be afraid of so long as I'm with you.'

Soon feeling better, she tried to disengage herself from my arm, but I held her all the tighter. My cheek was almost touching hers, and I knew that hers was burning. She said:

'Good God, what are you doing to me?'

I paid no attention to her trembling or to her confusion. My lips brushed her tender face. She shivered, but said nothing more. We were the last of the party, so no one could see. Having reached the farther bank we started to trot. The

PRINCESS MARY

princess would not give her horse its head, and I lagged behind with her. She was obviously troubled by my silence, but (being curious) I had determined not to utter a word. I wanted to see how she would extricate herself from so embarrassing a situation.

'Either you despise me, or else you are very much in love with me,' she said at length, in a voice broken with tears. 'Perhaps you are only amusing yourself with me, trying to break my heart and then forsake me. But that would be so base, so mean, I can hardly think it possible. Oh, no, it isn't true,' she went on, tenderly and trustfully. 'It can't be true that there is something in me which makes you despise me. Your audacious behaviour I must forgive, because I permitted it. Answer. Tell me. I want to hear your voice.'

There was so much feminine impatience in the last words that I couldn't help smiling. Luckily it was getting dark. I made no reply.

'Why don't you answer?' she went on. 'Perhaps you want me to say I love you, before you say you love me?'

I remained silent.

'Is that what you want?' she persisted, turning sharply to look at me. In her appearance and her voice there was something that alarmed me.

PRINCESS MARY

'Why should I want it?' I asked, shrugging my shoulders.

She gave her horse a cut with the whip, and went off at full gallop down the narrow, dangerous track. So suddenly was that done that I was unable to catch up with her before she reached the rest of the party. All the way to the gates of her house she was talking and laughing incessantly. Her movements had something feverish about them, and she did not once look at me. Everyone noticed her unusual cheerfulness. Her mother was obviously very much pleased, for she looked at Mary with delight. But Mary was only having a violent attack of nerves, so that I am sure that she will not sleep a wink tonight, but will cry most of the time. The thought fills me with pleasure—though at times I feel like a vampire. Yet I have the reputation of being a good fellow, and should like to sustain it.

Dismounting, the ladies entered the Ligovskys' house. Being agitated myself, I went for a gallop in the hills, hoping that the thoughts which were troubling me would be blown away. The dew was falling and the evening was intoxicatingly fresh. The dull beat of the unshod horse's hoofs echoed in the silence of the ravines. Having let my mount quench his thirst from a pool at the foot of a waterfall, I drew some deep breaths of the sweet southern air and started home. I rode through the suburb. The windows, many of them, were already dark. I could hear the calls of sentries on the ramparts, and the answering calls of Cossacks on picket duty near by.

In one of the suburban houses, a house built on the edge of a ravine, I noticed a very bright illumination. The discordant conversation and shouts which reached my ears from it now and again, showed that there must be a wine-party of officers there. I dismounted, hitched my horse, and walked quietly up to the window, which was but partly shuttered, so that I could see the revellers and hear what they were saying. They were talking about me.

The captain of dragoons, half-seas over, struck the table with his fist to demand attention.

'Gentlemen', he said. 'This has become insufferable. Pechorin must be taught a lesson. These fledglings from St. Petersburg always give themselves airs until someone tweaks their nose. He thinks that the world is his private preserve because he always wears clean gloves and well-polished boots.'

'Yes, and that arrogant smile of his,' said

PRINCESS MARY

another of the roysterers. 'But I wouldn't mind betting that he's a coward.'

'I think so too,' put in Grushnitsky. 'But he loves to turn matters off with a laugh. I once said something to him which would have made anyone else knock me down, but Pechorin treated it as a joke. The only reason I didn't challenge him was that the challenge had to come from him, and I didn't want to have anything to do with him.'

'Grushnitsky's in a wax with Pechorin because Pechorin has cut him out with young Princess Ligovsky.'

'That's all my eye,' said Grushnitsky. 'It's true that I was rather attracted by her, but I soon sheered off, because I don't want to marry, and it's against my principles to get a girl into trouble.'

'Oh, yes, I assure you he's a damned coward,' said the captain of dragoons. 'Pechorin I mean, of course, not Grushnitsky. Grushnitsky's all right. He's my intimate friend. Gentlemen, is there no one here to defend Pechorin? Not a soul? All the better. Would you like to test his courage? It would be amusing.'

'Of course we should like to. But how?'

'Listen. Grushnitsky, especially has his knife into Pechorin, so Grushnitsky shall play the chief part. Let him pick a quarrel and challenge Pechorin to a duel. Wait a minute. Here is the point. He challenges. Well then everything, the challenge, the preparations, the conditions, shall be solemn and intimidating. I'll arrange matters, for I shall be your second, my poor friend. Agreed? This is where the joke comes in. The pistols shall have charges of powder and wads, but no bullets. I know that Pechorin will be in a blue funk, for the duellists shall be only six paces apart. Deuce take it, a nasty-looking business. Do you agree, gentlemen?'

'A glorious idea.'—'Agreed.'—'Splendid.'— There was a chorus of approval.

'What do you say, Grushnitsky?'

I eagerly awaited his answer. Turning cold and hot by turns with anger, I realized that but for a lucky accident I should have been made the laughing-stock of these fools. If Grushnitsky had refused, I should have been ready to embrace him. But after a brief silence, he stood up, shook hands with the captain who had made the infamous proposal, and said pompously: 'Agreed.'

It would be hard to picture the delight of the honourable company.

On my way home I was torn by conflicting passions. One was regret. 'Why should they all hate me?' I thought. 'I've never been rude to any of them. Can I be one of the people whom everyone dislikes at sight?' But my other feeling was fierce anger, and this gradually became predominant. 'Watch out, Grushnitsky,' I said to myself a little later, as I paced up and down my rooms. 'I'm not a man to play with. You may have to pay dear for assenting to this scheme of your mutton-headed comrades.'

I could not sleep a wink, and by morning I was as yellow as an orange.

Princess Mary noticed it when she met me at the spring.

'Are you ill?' she asked, looking anxiously at me.

'I didn't sleep last night.'

'Nor did I,' she said. 'Perhaps I accused you wrongfully. Explain matters, and I'll forgive you everything.'

'Everything?'

'Everything, if you'll tell me the truth, without further delay. You see I've been thinking so hard, in the hope of justifying your behaviour. Perhaps you've been afraid that my relatives will make objections? That wouldn't matter. When they know' (her voice shook)— 'when they know, I shall be able to persuade them. Or are you thinking about your own

PRINCESS MARY

position? I could make any sacrifice for the man I love. Answer, answer quickly, and take pity on me. You don't despise me, do you?'

She grasped my hand.

Her mother was walking in front of us with Vera's husband, and saw nothing. But we were visible to the prowling invalids, who are prize scandalmongers, so I quickly freed my hand from her passionate clasp.

'I will tell you the whole truth,' I said to Mary, 'without trying to justify or explain my conduct; I don't love you.'

Her lips turned pale.

'Leave me,' she said, almost inaudibly.

With a shrug, I turned and left her.

June 25th. I sometimes regard myself with contempt. Is not that the reason why I despise others? I have become incapable of generous impulses; and am afraid of doing what may make me seem ridiculous to myself. Anyone else in my place would doubtless have offered Princess Mary his heart and his fortune, but on me the word 'marriage' has always had an uncanny magical effect. However passionately I may have loved a woman, directly she makes me feel that I ought to marry her, this means goodbye to love. My heart turns to stone as regards that woman, and nothing can soften it again where she is concerned. I could make any sacrifice except that of marrying. I would risk my life a dozen times on the turn of a card, would even risk my honour, but nothing will induce me to sell my freedom.

Why do I set so high a value on freedom? What use is it to me? For what am I striving? What do I expect in the future? To say sooth, nothing at all. Consequently my craving for freedom must be inborn, a sort of inexplicable prejudice. There are people who have an unaccountable fear of spiders, cockroaches, or mice. When I was a child an old frump who claimed to have second sight told my mother what was going to happen to me. A wicked woman would bring me to my death. This prophecy made a profound impression on me, and subsequently induced in me an intense aversion to marriage. Something tells me that what was foretold is really going to happen, but at least I can make every effort to postpone fulfilment as long as possible.

June 26th. A 'prestidigitator' named Apfelbaum arrived here yesterday. A long notice was posted on the doors of the restaurant, announcing that the above-named famous conjuror, acrobat, chemical and optical illusionist, was to give his magnificent performance today at eight o'clock in the fine assembly hall (read 'restaurant'). Price of admission two and a half roubles.

There was a general determination to go and see this distinguished conjuror. Even Princess Ligovsky took a ticket, though her daughter was ill.

After luncheon, I passed Vera's window. She was sitting alone on the balcony, and dropped a letter which fell at my feet. Here it is:

'Come to see me here this evening at ten, by the main staircase. My husband has gone to Pyatigorsk, and won't be back till tomorrow morning. The servants will all be out. I have given them tickets for the entertainment tonight, and the princess's people as well. I shall expect you. Come without fail.'

'Aha,' I thought, 'at last things are taking the turn I want.'

I went at eight to see the conjuror, but the hall did not fill up till towards nine, and then the show began. All Vera's and the princess's servants (men and women as well) were in the back rows. Grushnitsky was in the front row, with his lorgnette ready for use. The conjuror appealed to him when in want of a handkerchief, a watch, a ring, or what not.

Grushnitsky has cut me for some time. This evening he looked impudent whenever his eyes turned my way. I shan't forget this when the time comes to settle accounts.

At ten o'clock, I got up and left the hall.

Outside it was pitch-dark. The mountain tops were wrapped in cold, heavy clouds. Now and again a failing breeze stirred the poplars round the restaurant, near the windows of which was a crowd of people. Walking down the hill, I turned in at the gate, quickening my pace. Suddenly I thought I heard someone following me, so I pulled up and looked, but could discern nothing in the darkness. Still, to make sure I walked round the house. As I went past the young princess's window, I again heard footsteps behind me. Then a man wrapped in a cloak ran by. This was alarming, but I stole quietly to the main staircase and went up the dark stairs to the mezzanine. A door opened, and a little hand grasped mine.

'No one saw you?' whispered Vera, as she embraced me.

'No one.'

'Now will you believe that I love you? I hesitated so long, suffered so long—but you can do with me what you will.'

Her heart was beating violently, and her

hands were cold as ice. She began to voice grievances, made jealous complaints, asked me to confess everything, for (she said) she could bear my unfaithfulness with resignation, since she wanted nothing but my happiness. I did not fully believe her, but managed to calm her with vows of undying affection.

'So you aren't going to take Mary as your wife?' she said. 'You don't love her? She's madly in love with you, poor thing.'

At about two in the morning I opened the window and, having tied a couple of shawls together, let myself down from the upper veranda to the lower, holding on to a pillar. In the young princess's room, a light was still burning. This aroused my attention. The curtain was not fully drawn, so I was able to glance at the interior. Mary was sitting on her bed, clasping her knees. Her thick hair was covered by a lace nightcap, and on her white shoulders she wore a big crimson wrap, while her small feet were hidden in embroidered Persian slippers. She sat motionless, her head sunk on to her breast. On the table in front of her was an open book, which she was not reading, and the expression of her eyes was profoundly sad. Her thoughts were far away from the printed page which she must have scanned a hundred times.

PRINCESS MARY

At this moment someone moved behind a bush. I jumped from the veranda to the ground, and an invisible hand seized me by the shoulder.

'Aha,' said a harsh voice, 'I've caught you—the fellow who visits princesses by night.'

'Hold him,' said another man, springing out of a corner.

The two men were Grushnitsky and the captain of dragoons.

Knocking the latter down by giving him a sound blow on the head, I fled into the bushes. There I expected no difficulty, being well acquainted with the garden paths on the slope opposite our houses.

'Thieves! Turn out guard!' I heard them shout. A shot was fired, and a smoking wad fell close to my feet.

Within a minute I was back in my room, where I promptly undressed and got into bed. Hardly had my valet locked the door, when Grushnitsky and the captain of dragoons came and knocked loudly. The captain shouted:

'Pechorin, Pechorin, are you asleep? Are you there?'

'I was asleep, before you made that infernal clatter,' I answered angrily.

'Get up and help us. Thieves! Circassians!' they said.

'I've got a bad cold,' I growled, 'and am afraid of making it worse.'

They went away. I was sorry I had answered, since they might have spent a whole hour more looking for me in the garden. Meanwhile a frantic hubbub was going on outside. Cossacks galloped up from the fort. They were all hunting the 'robbers', beating the bushes in search of alleged Circassians, but found nobody. Still, many people remained firmly convinced that if the garrison had been braver and prompter two dozen robbers, at least, would have been laid out.

June 27th. At the spring this morning everyone talked about the night-attack by the Circassians. Having finished my ration of Narsan water, I was walking for the tenth time down the long poplar avenue when I met Vera's husband, who had just arrived from Pyatigorsk. He took my arm and we went together to the restaurant for lunch. I found he was much worried about his wife.

'She was terribly frightened last night,' he said. 'Just my luck that it should happen while I was away.'

We were sitting at a table near the doorway that leads into the corner room, where there were a dozen young men—among them Grushnitsky. For the second time I had the luck to overhear a conversation which was to decide his fate. He could not see me, so I had no reason to suppose that what he was saying was expressly aimed at me, but this made him all the more culpable.

'Were there really any Circassians last night?' asked someone. 'Who saw them?'

'I will tell you the actual facts,' answered Grushnitsky. 'But you must not give the show away. This is what happened. Yesterday a man whose name I must keep to myself came and informed me that at ten in the evening he had seen someone furtively enter the Ligovskys' house. Princess Ligovsky was here, at the conjuring performance, but Princess Mary was at home. I went with my informant to the window, and there we stayed on guard, to waylay the lucky fellow as he came out.'

I must admit that I was nervous, though my companion was busily occupied with his lunch, for I was afraid that he might hear something disagreeable to him if by chance Grushnitsky were to tumble on the truth, but, being blinded by jealousy, Grushnitsky never suspected in whose room I had actually been. He went on:

'We had taken a pistol with us, loaded with

powder only, simply to scare the intruder. We waited in the garden till two o'clock. At last he appeared, though the Lord knows where he actually came from. It was not out of the window, for that never opened, so it must have been through a glass door behind one of the pillars. But in the end we saw him jump down from the veranda. What about the princess, you ask? Well, you know what these Moscow ladies are like. We tried to seize him, but he eluded us and ran into the bushes like a hare. I fired my pistol at him as he disappeared.'

There was a murmur of incredulity from those who were listening to the story.

'You doubt me?' said the narrator. 'I give you my word of honour it's gospel truth. To prove it, if you like, I'll tell you his name.'

'Yes, tell us who it was,' said all of them with one voice.

'Pechorin,' answered Grushnitsky.

At this moment he raised his eyes. I had got up, and was standing in the door opposite to him. He flushed deeply. Going close to him I said slowly and clearly:

'I'm awfully sorry that I did not turn up before you pledged your word to this abominable slander. My presence might have hindered your uttering such an infamy.'

Grushnitsky rose in a fury, but I went on, no less quietly than before:

'I must ask you to recant your words without the smallest delay. You know perfectly well that you were lying. I hardly think that a woman's indifference to your shining virtues merited so terrible a vengeance. Think well and carefully. If you cling to what you said, you will forfeit all right to the name of honourable man—and you will risk your life.'

Grushnitsky stood facing me, eyes lowered, and violently agitated. But the struggle between conscience and vanity was soon over. The captain of dragoons, who was sitting close, gave him a nudge. Trembling, he answered quickly, though without looking up.

'My dear Sir, when I say a thing, it is what I really mean and what I am willing to repeat. I am not frightened by your threats, and am prepared for anything that may happen.'

'You have already shown as much,' I coldly replied, and taking the captain of dragoons by the arm I led him out of the room.

'What can I do for you?' asked the captain.

'You are Grushnitsky's friend, so I suppose you will be his second?'

The captain bowed stiffly.

'As you say,' he answered. 'It is incumbent on

PRINCESS MARY

me to be his second, for the insult to him is an insult to me also. It was I who kept watch with him last night,' went on the officer, drawing himself up.

'Ah, then it was you on whose head I barked my knuckles?'

He went yellow and blue by turns, but tried to restrain his indignation.

'My second will have the honour to call on you today,' I said, giving a formal bow as I went out, ignoring his furious look.

As I came to the staircase that leads into the restaurant, I met Vera's husband, who had obviously been waiting for me. He grasped my hand, shook it enthusiastically, and said with tears in his eyes:

'You are a fine young fellow. I heard everything. What scum they are. After this they ought not to be admitted into any decent home. Thank goodness I have no daughters. But she for whom you are risking your life will reward you. Rest assured of my discretion until the duel is over. I used to be young myself and I served in the army, so I know there must be no interference in these matters. Goodbye.'

Poor man. He was glad he had no daughters!

I went straight to Werner, whom I found at home, and I told him everything, not excepting my relations with Vera and Princess Mary, and the conversation I had overheard between the men who had wanted to fool me into fighting a duel in which the pistols would be loaded with nothing but powder. However the affair had certainly gone beyond a joke, and they had probably never expected any such development.

The doctor agreed to act as my second and I gave him some instructions as to the terms of the duel. He was to keep the affair as secret as possible, for though I did not mind facing death I was unwilling to have my career ruined.

Then I went home, and within an hour Werner rejoined me.

'There has certainly been a plot against you,' he said. 'At Grushnitsky's were the captain of dragoons and another man (whose name I have forgotten). I was outside the room for a minute, taking off my goloshes. The men were making a lot of noise, quarrelling.'

'"Certainly I shan't agree," said Grushnitsky. "He has publicly insulted me, and that has completely changed the position."

'"What's it got to do with you?" said the captain, "I take full responsibility. I've been second in five duels, and I know how matters ought to be arranged. I've thought of every-

PRINCESS MARY

thing, and you mustn't interfere. To frighten Pechorin will do him good. Why expose yourself to danger if it can be avoided?"

'At that moment I went in, and they stopped talking. We discussed matters for some time, and this is what we finally decided. About three miles from here is a deep ravine. They will ride out there tomorrow at four in the morning, and we shall follow half an hour later. You will stand six paces from one another. That was Grushnitsky's demand. If one of you is killed, it can be put down to the Circassians. Now let me tell you what has occurred to me. They have, I believe, altered their original plan, and intend to load one of the pistols with ball—Grushnitsky's. The other (yours) will have powder but no bullet. That looks uncommonly like murder, but in wartime, especially on the Asiatic border, tricks of the sort are by some considered allowable. Still, Grushnitsky, I fancy, is less dishonourable than his comrades. What do you think? Shall we show them we have tumbled to their game?'

'Not on any account, Doctor. Make your mind easy. I shan't let them lime me.'

'What do you propose to do, then?'

'I'll keep that to myself, if you don't mind.'

'Well, take care you aren't caught in their

snare. Remember you will be only six paces apart.'

'Werner, I shall expect you tomorrow at four. The horses shall be ready. Goodbye.'

I sat in my room till evening. A servant brought a message asking me to come to the Ligovskys', but I told him to say I wasn't well.

Two in the morning, and I've had no sleep yet. I must get some sleep to steady my hand, though it's not easy to miss at six paces. Grushnitsky, your mystification won't work. We shall change roles, and it will be my part to search your pale face for the signs of hidden fear. Why did you ask for that deadly nearness of six paces? Do you think me such a fool as to present my forehead for you to shoot at? We shall draw lots. But what if luck should be on his side? If my star should no longer shine? That may happen. It has shone unfailingly for so long.

Even so, if I die, I die. The world won't lose much, and I'm fairly bored by the world. I'm like a man yawning at a dance, whose only reason for not going home to sleep is that his carriage has not come yet. But if my carriage has come, good-night.

In memory I'm reliving my past, and I cannot

PRINCESS MARY

help asking myself what has been the meaning of my life, and why the devil I was ever born. I think there must have been a meaning, and that I must have had an important mission, for I feel that I have considerable strength of mind. But I have never been able to discover the mission, so I have succumbed to the temptation of futile and ungrateful passions. Out of the furnace of them I have issued hard and cold as steel, but I have hopelessly failed to pluck the most beautiful flower of life—the fire of noble impulses.

How often I have been no more than an axe in the hands of fate. Like a death-dealing instrument, I fell upon the heads of predestined victims, often without angry feeling, but always without regret.

My love has never brought anyone happiness, for I have never sacrificed anything for those I loved. I loved for myself, for my own pleasure. I was merely gratifying a strange need of my own heart, a greed for battening on others' feelings, on their tenderness for me, their joys and sufferings—and never did I gain full satisfaction. Like a man who falls asleep when exhausted and enervated by hunger, to dream of rich wines and savoury food, I have fancied myself freed from my distress. But then I have awakened to find the dream shattered, and to be plagued more than ever with hunger and despair.

Perhaps this morning I am to die. Then there will be no one in the world to form a sound view of me. Some will think too well of what I was; others too badly, deeming me worse than I really was. Some will say: 'He was a good fellow.' Others: 'He was a wretch.' They will all be wrong.

After this, is it worth while to go on living, or will it be too much trouble? Yet I know that if I can I shall go on living simply out of curiosity. For something new might happen. How absurd, and how annoying.

For six weeks I have been in the fort of N——. Maksim Maksimich is out shooting, and I am alone, sitting at the window. Grey clouds cover the mountains as far as the lower slopes. Through the mist the sun looks like a yellow smudge. It is cold. The wind whistles and makes the windows rattle. I feel distinctly bored, so I shall write up my diary again. It was interrupted by many strange happenings.

I have been reading the last page that was written. How absurd. I thought I was going to die. But that could not be, for I have not yet

PRINCESS MARY

drained the cup of suffering, and now I feel that I have a long life before me.

All that took place is clearly and sharply recorded in my memory. Not a line, not a shadow, has been effaced by time.

I remember that the night before the duel I did not get a wink of sleep. I was not able to go on writing, for a strange restlessness overcame me. For an hour I walked up and down the room, then I sat down and opened Walter Scott's *Old Mortality* which was lying on my table. I read it at first with difficulty, but soon I became immersed in it, carried away by the author's marvellous inventive faculty.

At length dawn came, and I found I was less nervous. I looked at myself in the mirror. My face was ashen pale, and furrowed with the lines of sleeplessness; but, my eyes, though they had dark shadows under them, shone steadily. I was well content.

Having given orders for the horses to be saddled, I slipped on a dressing-gown and went to the bathroom. When I had plunged into a tub filled with cold, sparkling Narsan water, I felt bodily and mental strength return; and got out of the bath fresh and vigorous, as if I were about to dress for a ball. Yet we are often told that the mind is not dependent on the body.

PRINCESS MARY

When I got back to my room, I found Werner there. He had on grey riding-breeches, a short Caucasian overcoat, and a Circassian cap. I burst out laughing at the sight of his small frame beneath this huge, shaggy cap. His features were by no means those of a warrior, and his face looked longer than ever.

'Why are you so glum, Doctor?' I asked. 'Haven't you accompanied people with the utmost equanimity hundreds of times already when they were on their way to the other world? Suppose I had diphtheria? I might get better, I might die. Either would be possible. Both would be in the order of things. Try to look on me as a patient in the grip of an illness you have not yet diagnosed. Then your curiosity will be roused, and you may be able to make some important physiological observations. Surely the expectation of a violent death is itself a sort of disease?'

Werner was struck by the force of this notion, and he cheered up.

We mounted our horses. The doctor gripped his reins with both hands, and we set forth. We speedily passed the fort, got through the adjoining suburb, and continued along the ravine up which our road led. It was half overgrown with long grass, and frequently crossed the noisy torrent, which we had to ford, much to

Werner's disgust, since his mount had a way of halting in mid stream.

I cannot remember another morning on which the sky was so blue and the air so invigorating. The sun was only just beginning to show itself behind the green hilltops, and the mingling of its warm rays with the chill of the disappearing night aroused a feeling of delightful languor in all my senses. The light had not yet fully reached the bottom of the valley, but gilded the crests of the overhanging rocks on either side of our route. At the least breath of wind, the thick bushes that sprang from the crevices besprinkled as with silvery dew-drops. My love of nature, I recall, became stronger than ever before. I watched each rainbow-tinted drop as it quivered on the broad leaves, and scattered millions of polychrome rays. My gaze eagerly endeavoured to pierce the hazy distance. Our road narrowed as the eye traced its course, amid rocks that became bluer and more precipitous, till they seemed to meet in an impenetrable wall. On we went in silence, which Werner broke at last by saying:

'Pechorin, have you made your will?'

'No.'

'But what will happen if you're killed?'

'An intestate's heirs will present themselves.'

PRINCESS MARY

'Surely you must have friends to whom you would like to send a farewell message?'

I shook my head.

'Is there not a woman somewhere to whom you would gladly communicate a last greeting?'

'Do you want me to lay my soul bare to you? Look here, old chap, I've got beyond the age when a man dies with a woman's name on his lips, or bequeathes to a friend a lock of hair which is perhaps greasy with pomatum. When I contemplate the imminence of death, I think only of myself. Other men may behave differently. Friends will forget me tomorrow, or (worse still) will weave all sorts of fictions about me; women, in some other man's arms, will mock my memory lest they should make a new lover jealous. Well, God be with them all. The storms of life have left me a few ideas, but have stripped me bare of feelings. For a long time, now, I have guided my life by my head, not by my heart. I appraise and interpret my passions and my actions with much curiosity, but in a spirit of aloofness. There are two personalities within me: one who lives in the fullest sense of the word; another who thinks about and criticizes the first. Number one will perhaps say goodbye to you and the world within the hour. Number two . . .

PRINCESS MARY

'Look, Doctor, are not there three black figures on the rocks to the right? Our adversaries, I expect, who are waiting for us.'

We quickened our pace.

At the foot of the rock three horses were hitched to the bushes. Having made ours fast in the same place, we climbed a narrow path to the level top where Grushnitsky was awaiting us with the captain of dragoons and another second who was introduced as Ivan Ignatevich. I never learned his surname.

'You've kept us waiting rather a long time,' said the captain, with a sardonic smile.

I pulled out my watch, and pointed to the dial. We had arrived on the tick, and he admitted that he was probably fast.

An embarrassing silence followed. Then Werner turned to Grushnitsky and said:

'Now that you have both shown your willingness to exchange shots, surely we can consider that honour is satisfied? Don't you think, gentlemen, you can make explanations to one another, and thus settle matters amicably?'

'I am willing,' was my answer to this proposal.

The captain winked at Grushnitsky, who, fancying I must be in a funk, assumed an arrogant air, though hitherto he had been deadly pale. For the first time since our arrival he raised his eyes to look at me, and I could discern in him a restlessness which disclosed an inward struggle.

'State your conditions,' he said, 'and you can be sure that I will do anything I can to meet you.'

'Here they are—simple enough. I want you to retract your slander in public this very day, and to beg my pardon.'

'I am amazed that you dare to suggest any such thing.'

'What else could you expect?'

'In that case the duel must go on.

I shrugged, and said:

'As you please, but remember that if so one of us will inevitably be killed.'

'I hope it may be you.'

'I can assure you of the contrary.'

He grew confused, flushed, and forced a laugh.

The captain took his arm and led him aside. They had a long conversation, in whispers. I had grown fairly peaceable, but this delay was beginning to annoy me.

The doctor came up to me. He spoke with manifest anxiety.

'Look here, Pechorin, you seem to have for-

PRINCESS MARY

gotten all about their plot. I shan't be able to load your pistol, and in that case. . . . You're a queer fellow. If you tell them you know of their conspiracy, they'll be afraid to carry it out. Theirs is a devilish plan, to shoot you down like a bird.'

'Please don't worry, Werner. You need only wait a little. I shall manage things in such a way that they will gain no advantage. Give them time to whisper.'

However, after a while I said:

'Gentlemen, this is growing tedious. If we're to fight, let's fight. Surely you had leisure for talking yesterday?'

'We're ready,' answered the captain. 'Gentlemen, to your places, please. Doctor, measure the distance, won't you? Six paces.'

'Go ahead, gentlemen,' repeated Ivan Ignatevich, in a small, piping voice.

'Excuse me,' I intervened. 'There's one more point to consider. Since this is to be a fight to the death, we must do what we can to keep things secret, lest our seconds should be held accountable. Do you agree?'

'Agreed, agreed,' they all said.

'Well, then, here's my proposal. You can see a small piece of flat ground on the top of that precipitous rock to the right there? There's a drop of two hundred feet, or perhaps more, and at the bottom lie sharp stones. Each of us will stand close to the precipice and then even a trifling wound will prove fatal. I'm sure that's what you want, since you have proposed we should open the duel when only six paces apart. The wounded duellist will instantly fall down the precipice and be dashed to pieces. The doctor need merely extract the bullet, and it will be easy to explain that death was due to an unlucky stumble. We will toss up to decide who shall fire first. Those are my conditions. You can take them or leave them.'

'Very well,' said the captain, with a significant look at Grushnitsky, who nodded in token of assent. My adversary's expression was continually changing. I had put him in a very awkward position. If we had been going to exchange shots on ordinary ground, he could have aimed at one of my legs, where a slight wound would have satisfied his desire for vengeance without putting too great a strain on his conscience. Now he must either fire in the air; or murder me; or else, abandoning his base design, meet me on equal terms and exposed to no less danger than myself. It would not have suited me at all to be in his shoes. He took the captain aside, and talked heatedly, while his lips were

PRINCESS MARY

blue and trembled. But the captain turned from him with a smile of contempt.

'You damned fool,' I heard him say. 'You don't in the least understand.—Gentlemen, let's begin.'

The narrow path to our chosen platform was a steep ascent through bushes. Fragments of rock functioned as precarious steps to this natural staircase. We scrambled up holding on to the bushes. Grushnitsky went first, followed by his seconds. The doctor and I brought up the rear.

'I'm amazed at you,' said Werner, grasping my hand. 'Let me feel your pulse. . . . Ah, you're rather feverish. Still, there's practically no sign of fever in your face, though your eyes are brighter than usual.'

Suddenly some small stones rushed past our feet with a rattle. What was it? Grushnitsky had lost his footing. The branch he was holding on to snapped. He would have fallen backwards, had not his seconds supported him.

'Watch out,' I called to him. 'Don't tumble down too soon. Remember what happened to Julius Caesar, who had the falling sickness.'

Then we made our way to the top of the precipitous rock, where the level was covered with a thin layer of sand. The very place for a duel.

All around were mountain tops, disappearing into the golden morning mist, an innumerable herd of them; while to the south Elbruz displayed his vast white expanse, completing the ring of snowy summits, between which hovered fleecy clouds, blown up from the east. Going to the edge of the plateau I looked down, and nearly turned giddy, for below me it was as dark and cold as a tomb, where moss-grown crags, detached by thunder and time, were awaiting their prey.

The plateau on which we were to fight our duel was an almost equilateral triangle. Six paces were measured from one of the angles, where it was agreed that the man at whom the first shot was to be fired should stand for the purpose. If he escaped death, his antagonist was to change places with him.

I had decided to give Grushnitsky every possible advantage. I wanted to test him. Perhaps he would show a spark of generosity, and then everything could be arranged for the best. But more probably his vanity and weakness of character would triumph. I hoped to feel that I should have full right to show him no mercy if fate should spare me. Who is there that has not bargained in this way with his conscience?

'Toss a coin, Doctor,' said the captain.

PRINCESS MARY

Werner took a piece of silver from his pocket, put it on his thumbnail, and spun it into the air.

'Tails,' shouted Grushnitsky, like a man who has been roused by a friendly push.

'Heads,' I exclaimed.

The coin rose, and then fell on the ground with a clink. We all ran up to look at it.

'You're in luck,' I said to Grushnitsky. 'It's tails, so you will fire first. But remember that if you don't kill me I can promise you that I shan't miss.'

He flushed, being ashamed to shoot an unarmed man. For a moment I fancied he was going to fling himself at my feet and implore forgiveness. But how could he confess the treachery he had planned? There was another way out for him. He could fire in the air; and I was almost certain he would do that. Only one thing would restrain him, the thought that I might demand a second duel.

'Time!' whispered Werner, clutching my sleeve.

'If you don't say you are aware of their plot, everything will be lost. Look, he's loading. If you won't speak, I will.'

'Not on any account, Doctor,' I replied, plucking him back by the arm. 'You'll spoil my game. You promised that you wouldn't interfere. After all, what's it got to do with you? Perhaps I want to be killed.'

He looked at me in amazement, saying:

'Oh, well, if that's so, it's another kettle of fish. Only don't complain of me when you get to the other world.'

Meanwhile the captain had loaded the pistols, and he gave one to Grushnitsky, whispering as he did so. Then he handed the other pistol to me.

Taking my stand in the appointed angle, I braced my left leg against a stone, and leaned forward a little, in the hope that if I received no more than a slight wound I should not fall backward.

Grushnitsky stood facing me and, at a given signal, began to raise his pistol. His knees were shaking, but he aimed squarely at my forehead. Inexplicable fury seized me. Suddenly he lowered the barrel of his pistol and, turning white as a sheet, he said hoarsely to his second:

'I can't do it.'

'Coward,' answered the captain.

A shot rang out. The bullet grazed my knee. Automatically I stepped forward, to get away from the edge as soon as possible.

'It's a pity you missed, Grushnitsky,' said the captain. 'Now it's your turn to be shot at. Get

PRINCESS MARY

ready. But embrace me first, for we shan't meet again.' They flung their arms round one another, and the captain could hardly keep from grinning. 'Don't be afraid,' he added, with a sly glance at Grushnitsky. 'The world's all nonsense. Nature's a fool. Fate is an idiot. Life is not worth a farthing.'

Having said his piece, with a solemnity worthy of its tragic meaning, the captain went to his place. Ivan Ignatevich, with tears in his eyes, also embraced Grushnitsky, who, going to the angle, stood alone facing me.

Since then I have vainly tried to understand the precise nature of the emotion which seized me at this juncture. There was the annoyance that results from wounded self-love, mingled with contempt and hatred aroused by the thought that this man who now faced me with such quiet effrontery had, two minutes before, tried to kill me like a dog—for if the wound in my leg had been only a very little more severe I should inevitably have fallen from the rock.

For a little while I looked him steadily in the face trying to discover the smallest sign of repentance. But it seemed to me that he was hiding a smile.

'I advise you to pray to God before you die,' I said to him.

PRINCESS MARY

'Don't trouble about my soul any more than about your own. I only ask you one favour. Shoot quickly, and have done with it.'

'Will you not retract your slander and beg my pardon? Think carefully. Does your conscience prick you?'

'Pechorin,' shouted the captain of dragoons, 'allow me to remark that you did not come here to preach a sermon. Let us finish quickly. Someone may ride up the valley and see us.'

'All right. Doctor, please come here.'

Werner came. Poor fellow, he was paler than Grushnitsky had been ten minutes before.

Then, speaking loudly and clearly, as a judge pronounces a sentence of death, I said:

'Doctor, these gentlemen, no doubt because they were in a hurry, have forgotten to load my pistol properly. There's no bullet in it. I beg you to reload it.'

'Impossible,' shouted the captain. 'Utterly impossible. I put a bullet in each pistol, and I suppose the bullet has dropped out of yours. That's no fault of mine. You've no right to have yours reloaded, no right at all. It's against the rules, and I shan't permit it.'

'As you please,' I said. 'But in that case I'll fight you on the same conditions.'

To this he hadn't a word to say.

PRINCESS MARY

Grushnitsky stood with his head hanging on his chest. He looked confused and miserable.

'Let them be,' he said at last to the captain, who was trying to snatch my pistol from the doctor's hands. 'You know they are perfectly right.'

Vainly the captain made signs to Grushnitsky, who refused to look at him.

The doctor loaded the pistol and handed it to me.

Seeing this, the captain spat and stamped.

'You're a fool,' he said to Grushnitsky. 'An utter fool. You had entrusted matters to me, and ought to have obeyed me in everything. Serves you right, now; you'll be squashed like a fly.'

Then he turned away, muttering:

'All the same, it's absolutely against the rules.'

'Grushnitsky,' I protested, 'there's still time. Retract your slander, and I'll forgive you everything. You didn't succeed in making a fool of me, and my vanity is appeased. Remember, we used to be friends.'

His face lit up and his eyes flashed.

'Shoot,' he said. 'I despise and hate you. If you don't kill me, I shall lie in wait some night, and make an end of you with a dagger. There's not room for both of us in this world.'

PRINCESS MARY

I fired.

When the smoke cleared off, Grushnitsky had vanished. At the edge of the precipice there was nothing to be seen but a faint column of dust.

Everyone except me screamed.

'The comedy is over. Ring down the curtain,' I said to Werner.

He made no reply, but turned away in horror.

I shrugged my shoulders, and said goodbye to Grushnitsky's seconds.

As I went down the path. I saw my adversary's dead body, which had lodged in a crevice among the rocks. Involuntarily I shut my eyes.

Untethering my horse, I mounted and rode homeward at a foot's pace. My heart felt as heavy as lead. The sun seemed dim, and its rays did not warm me.

Before reaching the suburb, I turned to the right up a ravine. The thought of meeting anyone was unbearable. I wanted above all to be alone. Dropping the reins and hanging my head, I went on a long way, and at length reached a place which was quite unknown to me. Here I turned my horse and found the way home. The sun was setting when I reached Kislovodsk, as tired and hungry as the beast I was riding.

My valet told me that Werner had called. He

handed me two letters, one from the doctor, the other from Vera.

I opened the first. It ran as follows:

'All has turned out well. We recovered the body, which is not much disfigured. The bullet was in the thorax. I extracted it. The general belief is that death was due to a sad accident. The colonel, who had probably heard about your quarrel, shook his head when told this story, but said nothing to the contrary. There is no evidence against you, and you may sleep quietly—if you can. Farewell.'

I hesitated a long time before opening the second letter. What could she have written to me about? The thought was most oppressive.

At length I read it, and every word is engraved indelibly on my mind:

'I write to you, fully believing that we shall never meet again. Some years ago, when we parted, I believed the same thing; but Heaven thought fit to send me this further trial. I did not withstand temptation, and my weak heart yielded once more to the familiar voice. You surely will not despise me for that? This letter is at one and the same time a farewell and a confession. I feel impelled to tell you all that has filled my heart since I began to love you. I shall not blame you, for you did with me what any other man would have done. You loved me as your property; as the fount of the joys, the anxieties, and the griefs that succeeded one another in you, the feelings without which life would have been dull and monotonous. I understood that from the beginning. But you were unhappy, and I sacrificed myself in the vain hope that some day you would value my sacrifice, that some day you would understand my deep tenderness, which was independent of external conditions. Much water has run under the bridges since then, and I have penetrated the inmost secrets of your heart. I have learned that my hope was vain. Oh, that was bitter. But my love for you had become part of me, and though it waned it did not die.

'We are now parting for ever, but you may rest assured that I shall never love another man. My heart has lavished on you all its treasures, all its tears, and all its hopes. Having loved you, I shall never regard other men without disdain. Not because you are better than they. No, but in you there is a quality peculiar to yourself, something masterful and mysterious. In your voice, no matter what you may be saying, there is overwhelming power; no one else can have such an unceasing desire to be loved, and in no one else is evil so attractive. No one else's eyes promise so much happiness; nor can anyone else be so genuinely unhappy, for no one else tries so hard to convince himself that he is happy.

'Now I must tell you why I am going away. The reason will not seem to you important, for it concerns myself alone.

'This morning my husband came into my room and told me of your quarrel with Grushnitsky. The expression of my face must have changed very much while he was speaking. I know this because he looked so long and steadily into my eyes. I nearly fainted at the thought that you were fighting a duel, and that I was the cause of it. I felt as if I were going mad. But now that I have been able to pull myself together, I am sure that you will not be killed. It is impossible that you can die while I remain alive. My husband walked up and down the room for a long time. I don't know what he said to me, nor can I remember my answers. I probably told him that I love you. The only thing that I am sure of is that towards the end of our conversation he called me an abominable name, and then went out. I heard him order the carriage. For the last three hours I have been sitting at the window, waiting for you to come back from the duel. But I am sure you are alive. You cannot die yet. The carriage is nearly ready. Goodbye, goodbye. I am ruined—but what does that matter? If I could only be sure that you will never forget me; I will not say, go on loving me, but merely remember me. Farewell. They are coming. I must hide this letter.

'It is not true, is it, that you love Mary? You will not marry her? Listen, you must make this sacrifice for me, when I have given up the world for you.'

I rushed downstairs like a madman, jumped into the saddle, for my horse was still in the yard, and galloped off down the road to Pyatigorsk. Unmercifully I lashed him, tired though he was, so that, panting and in a lather of sweat, he carried me along the stony road.

The sun was already hiding behind a black cloud which overhung the western ridge of the mountains. The gorge was dark and damp. The Podkumok, as it coursed along its stony bed, uttered a hollow, monotonous roar. I continued to gallop, for I was so impatient that I could hardly breathe. The thought that I might not find her at Pyatigorsk was belabouring my heart with blows like those of a sledgehammer. I yearned to see her for a minute, just one more minute, and then to say farewell with a shake of the hand. Prayers, curses, tears, laughter—

PRINCESS MARY

nothing could adequately express the turmoil of my despair. Now that I seemed likely to lose her for ever, Vera had instantly become the most precious thing in the world—dearer than life, honour, or happiness. God alone knows what strange tempestuous thoughts raced through my head. All the time I went on galloping, and mercilessly flogged my horse. Then I noticed that he had become frightfully short of breath, and twice he stumbled on level ground. But it was only three miles more to Esentuki, a Cossack village where I hoped to get a fresh mount.

All would have been well if the poor beast's strength had held out for another ten minutes, but as I came through a place where the gorge narrowed before the stream got clear of the mountains, at a sharp turn he suddenly fell. Jumping clear, I tugged at the reins and tried to make him get up. No good. Some barely audible grunts issued from between his teeth which were clenched on the bit. Then, very soon, he died. Now that I was left alone my last hope was gone. I tried to walk on, but my legs gave way under me. Worn out by the anxieties of the day and by want of sleep, I fell into the wet grass and cried like a child.

Long I lay there motionless, sobbing, not

even making an effort to restrain my tears. I felt as if my lungs would burst. My firmness, my cold self-command, had vanished like smoke. Reason was dumb. I had no strength left. If anyone had seen me in the condition, he would have turned contemptuously away.

When the dews of nightfall and the chill breeze from the mountains had cooled my burning head, my thoughts began to clear, and I realized that the pursuit of my lost happiness was futile. What had driven me on the chase? The wish to see her. Why? Was not all ended between us? A bitter farewell kiss would not enrich my memories, but would only make parting more difficult.

For some reason I was glad that I had been able to weep. I suppose the crying fit was the outcome of lacerated nerves, of a sleepless night, and of an empty stomach—to say nothing of facing a pistol for two minutes.

All was for the best. This new suffering would serve (as a soldier might put it) to distract my attention from the old. It had done me good to cry, and besides, if I had not ridden furiously in pursuit of Vera, and then been compelled to walk ten miles home, I should probably have passed another sleepless night. When I got back to Kislovodsk at five in the morning, I threw myself on the bed and slept as soundly as Napoleon is said to have slept after Waterloo.

When I awoke, night had already come again. I sat at the open window and flung my coat wide, to let the fresh mountain breeze blow on my chest, for the heavy sleep of exhaustion had not fully restored me. In the distance beyond the river, through the leafy tops of the poplars that shaded its banks, lamps in the fort and in the suburb were twinkling. In the yard close at hand all was still, and the princess's windows were unlighted.

Werner came in. He was frowning and (contrary to his usual habit) did not shake hands.

'Where do you come from, Doctor?'

'From Princess Ligovsky's. Her daughter is ill—suffering from an attack of nerves. But I did not come here to talk about that. The authorities suspect you to have caused Grushnitsky's death, and though they can't prove anything you had better be on guard. Princess Ligovsky told me today she knew you had fought a duel in defence of her daughter's reputation. That old fellow blabbed everything to her. What was his name? I mean the man who witnessed your quarrel with Grushnitsky in the restaurant. I came to warn you. Goodbye.

Maybe we shan't meet again. They'll probably send you off somewhere.'

On the threshold he paused, for he wanted to shake hands. If I had shown the slightest inclination to respond, he would have cordially embraced me. But I sat as cold as a stone, and he went out.

That's what people are—all alike. They know beforehand the seamy side of an action; they will help, advise you to do it, and even give vigorous support, knowing there is no other possible line to take. But when it is done, they wash their hands of the whole affair, and indignantly turn against the man who has had the courage to take the responsibility for it. All cut on the same pattern, even the best, even the most intelligent.

Next morning, having received orders from the authorities to betake myself to Fort N——, I went to the Ligovskys' to bid goodbye.

Princess Ligovsky asked whether I had anything particularly important to tell her. Evading the issue, I wished her every happiness and so on.

'Well,' she said, 'I have something very serious to talk to you about.'

I made no reply.

She obviously did not know how to begin.

PRINCESS MARY

Turning livid, she thrummed on the table with her puffy fingers. At length she spoke, haltingly.

'Listen, Monsieur Pechorin, I believe you to be an honourable man.'

I bowed in acknowledgment, but made no answer. She went on.

'I am quite sure you are an honourable man, although your behaviour is somewhat questionable. But you may have excellent reasons for that behaviour. I do not know them, and should like you to tell me. You defended my daughter against a slander, fought a duel for this purpose, thus risking your life. Please make no answer, for you will not wish to admit having fought the duel, since Grushnitsky is dead.' (She crossed herself.) 'God forgive him, and you too, I hope. That affair is no concern of mine, and I dare not pass judgment on you for what you did, seeing that my daughter was the innocent cause of the duel. She told me everything, at least I think so—how you informed her you were in love with her, and she said she was in love with you.' (The princess sighed deeply.) 'But she is ill, and I am convinced that it is no ordinary illness. Some secret grief afflicts her. She will not admit it, but I am sure that you are the cause. Listen to me. You may think that I want to secure for her rank or wealth. If so, you are wrong. I value nothing but my daughter's happiness. Your present position is not very grand, but it may improve. You have private means, and you love my daughter. She has been brought up in such a way as to make her husband happy. I am well-to-do, and she is my only daughter. What holds you back? I know I ought not to talk to you in this way, but I trust your heart and your honour. Let me repeat that she is my only child.'

Princess Ligovsky burst into tears.

'Look here, Princess,' I said, 'it is impossible for me to reply to you. Let me speak to your daughter alone.'

'Never,' she exclaimed, rising in great agitation.

'As you please,' I said, moving to depart.

After a moment's reflection, she waved to me to sit down again, and went out of the room.

Five minutes passed. My heart beat forcibly, but my mind was clear and my head was cool. Within I searched for the least spark of love for this charming girl who was being offered me in marriage, but could not find a trace of anything of the sort.

The door opened, and she came in. God, how she had changed since I last saw her.

Walking to the middle of the room, she tot-

PRINCESS MARY

tered and nearly fell. I jumped up, took her by the arm, and led her to a chair.

I stood facing her, and for a long time neither of us spoke. Her big eyes, incredibly sad, seemed to be searching mine for something that would give her a glimpse of hope. With pallid lips she tried in vain to smile. Her tender hands, clasped on her knees, looked so thin and transparent that I was touched with pity.

'Princess,' I said, 'you know that I was amusing myself at your expense. You must despise me.'

A hectic flush tinged her cheeks. I went on:

'That being so, it is impossible you can love me.'

She turned away, rested her elbows on the table, covering her eyes with her hands—but not before I had seen tears.

'O God!' she said, almost inaudibly.

This began to be more than I could bear. Another minute, and I should have flung myself at her feet. I resumed, however, speaking as firmly and resolutely as I could:

'So you must see for yourself that I cannot possibly marry you. Even if now you wanted me to, you would soon change your mind. My talk with your mother has made it necessary for me to explain matters to you candidly, without circumlocution. I hope she is mistaken. Then it will be easy for you to undeceive her. You see that in your eyes I am playing an odious and contemptible part. I acknowledge it freely, and that is all I can do for you. However unfavourable your opinion of me, I bow to it. I abase myself before you. Even if you did love me, surely by now love must have given place to contempt?'

She turned to me white as marble, her eyes flashing strangely.

'I hate you,' she said.

Bowing respectfully, I left the room.

An hour afterwards a swift troika was whirling me away from Kislovodsk. A few miles from Esentuki I saw the carcass of my good horse by the roadside. His saddle had been removed, no doubt by passing Cossacks. Two crows were perched on his back. Sighing, I looked the other way.

Here, in this wearisome fort, I often review the past, and ask myself why I was unwilling to tread the road opened to me by fate, a road where gentle pleasures and peace of mind awaited me. But no, I could never have become reconciled to it. I am like a seaman who was born and bred on the deck of a pirate ship. He has become so accustomed to storms and battles that on land he feels insufferably bored, however alluring the shady woods, however temperate the sunshine. All day long he haunts the shore, listening to the rhythmic murmur of the breaking waves and looking into the misty distance. At last, gleaming on the dim line of the horizon that lies between the blue sea and the grey clouds, he sees the sail for which he yearns. At first it is like a seagull's wing, but little by little the ship stands out from the foam of the breakers, and with an even keel, approaches the deserted quay.

A FATALIST

A FATALIST

I WAS once stationed for a fortnight with a battalion of infantry in a Cossack village on our left flank. In the evenings the officers assembled in one another's quarters, turn and turn about, to while away the time over cards.

One day at Major S——'s, getting bored with Boston, we threw the cards under the table and sat up late, talking. The conversation was interesting, which was unusual. We discussed the Mohammedan doctrine of kismet, the doctrine that man's fate is written in heaven, and found that among us it had many votaries. Each of us gave some illustration which told in favour of it or against it.

'But none of that proves anything, gentlemen,' said the old major. 'Not one of you personally saw the strange happenings on which you base your opinions.'

'Of course not,' some of them agreed. 'But we heard of them from trustworthy persons.'

'Stuff and nonsense,' put in one of those present. 'Where are the trustworthy persons who have seen the writing which foretold the hour of someone's death? If predestination really exists, why do we have free will, and why do we reason? Why are we held answerable for our actions?'

At this moment one of the officers who had been sitting in a corner of the room got up and walked slowly to the table, looking at us all quietly and seriously. He was a Serb, as was evident from his name.

Lieutenant Vulich's appearance was in strict conformity with his character. A tall man, he had a dark skin, black hair, black and piercing eyes, and a big, straight nose—this being a peculiarity of his race. A cold and melancholy smile hovered unceasingly on his lips. All these points were combined to make him look like one set apart, unable to share his thoughts and feelings with those whom fortune had made his companions. He was courageous; seldom spoke, but when he did speak it was to good effect; and he never gabbled about personal or family secrets. He rarely touched wine; and as for the young Cossack women, whose charms do not appeal to strangers, he left them strictly alone. It was said, however, that the colonel's wife was by no means indifferent to his expressive eyes, but any allusions to this annoyed him very much.

He had one passion which he could not hide,

A FATALIST

a craze for gambling. Beside a gaming-table covered with green cloth, he lost count of everything else. His luck was bad, but losses only stimulated his desire to play. The story ran that once when he was on active service, they were playing banker at night, and he was having a run of luck. Suddenly shots were heard, the alarm was sounded, and almost everyone, of course, jumped up and ran for sword and pistols. 'Stake before you go,' shouted Vulich to one of the most zealous punters. 'I choose seven,' quoth the latter, and rushed off. Despite the general hubbub, Vulich finished the deal, and seven won.

When he turned up at the front, the firing was general. But regardless of bullet or sword, he went on hunting for the punter whose card had won. Having found the man in the firing-line where the enemy was being driven out of a wood, Vulich shouted, 'Your seven won,' and drew some notes out of his pocket. The holder of the winning card protested that this was an ill time for settling such debts, but had to accept payment willy-nilly. Having thus discharged the obligation, the gambler rushed forward to the head of his men, and fought calmly till the action was over.

When, on the occasion of this talk about

A FATALIST

kismet, Lieutenant Vulich came to the table, no one spoke; we all waited, expecting him to do something original.

'Gentlemen,' he began, in a voice that was quiet, but pitched lower than usual, 'these arguments seem to me unmeaning. You want proof. I am prepared to make an experiment on myself—an experiment which will show clearly whether a man can decide to end his life when he pleases, or whether the fatal moment is "written" for us all. Shall I go ahead?'

'No'—'No'—'No'—came as an almost universal chorus. The proposal seemed to most of us too queer, too uncanny.

'I'll make a bet with you,' said I, in jest.

'What is your bet?'

'I'll wager that amount to defend the thesis that there's no such thing as predestination,' I said, flinging sixty roubles on the table. That was all the money I had in my pocket.

'Done,' replied Vulich. 'Major, you shall be umpire. Hold the stakes. Here are fifty roubles. Perhaps you'll lend me ten to make up an even bet, since I've no more cash on me?'

'Certainly,' said the major. 'But I can't for the life of me see how you're going to decide.'

Without a word Vulich went into the major's bedroom, whither we followed him. Going up

A FATALIST

to the wall, on which hung various pistols, he took down one at random. We still did not understand, but when he primed and cocked it we seized his arm and one of us shouted:

'What the devil are you up to? You must have gone crazy.'

'Gentlemen,' he said slowly, freeing his arm, 'which of you wants to pay the sixty roubles that will be due from me if I lose my bet?'

Silently we all returned to the card-room.

He came back too, and sat down at the table. We sat likewise, in a circle, as he directed with a wave of the hand. We obeyed, for he seemed to radiate a mysterious influence. I looked steadily into his eyes; he countered my inquisitive gaze without wavering, and his pale lips parted in a smile. Nevertheless, for all his self-possession, it seemed to me that I could discern the seal of death upon his white face. I have noticed (and many experienced campaigners will substantiate this) that when a man is doomed to die within a few hours the strange signs of his inevitable doom can often be read from his countenance. Those who have practical knowledge in such matters will rarely be mistaken.

I said to him:

'You are going to die today.'

A FATALIST

He turned his face towards me with a jerk, but answered slowly and quietly:

'Perhaps so, perhaps not. Time will show.'

Then, turning to the major, he asked:

'Is this pistol loaded?'

The major said he could not positively remember.

Someone else called out:

'Dry up, Vulich. Of course it's loaded, and you can blow out your brains with it if you choose to try. Is this a joke?'

'A poor joke,' said another.

Yet another: 'I'll lay you fifty roubles to five that it's not loaded.'

'Done,' said Vulich again.

I was getting bored by all this talk, so I intervened, saying:

'Listen to me, either fire the pistol, or hang it up where it was and let's go home to bed.'

'Yes,' exclaimed many of the others. 'He's right. It's past bedtime. We'll toddle.'

'Gentlemen,' replied Vulich, 'please don't go yet,' and he raised the pistol to his forehead. They were all horrified. 'Pechorin,' he went on, 'will you kindly draw a card and throw it up into the air?'

I did as he requested. The card (as far as I can remember) was the ace of hearts. All held

A FATALIST

their breath. Their eyes, betraying both fear and vague curiosity, turned from the pistol to the fateful card, which fell fluttering. As it touched the table, Vulich pulled the trigger. A click followed, but no bang.

'Thank God, the pistol wasn't loaded after all,' cried most of those present.

'We'll see about that,' said Vulich.

Having recocked the pistol, he aimed at a cap hanging by the window, and fired. There was a loud report, and the room filled with smoke. As soon as the air had cleared, the cap was examined. A hole had been bored through the very middle, and the bullet had buried itself deep in the wall.

For two or three minutes, no one had a word to say. Vulich quietly pocketed my sixty roubles.

Then there came a lot of discussion as to why the pistol had not gone off the first time the hammer fell. Some contended it was probable that the priming pan was fouled. Others, whispering, declared that the powder might have been damp, and had then been renewed. But I knew that this last idea was false, for my eyes had never left the pistol.

'You're in luck tonight,' I said to Vulich.

'Yes, for once,' he answered, with a smile of

A FATALIST

satisfaction. 'This game suits me better than banker or hazard.'

'Praps a trifle more dangerous,' I could not help saying.

'What, are you beginning to believe in predestination?'

'Yes. But I don't understand why I thought your end was coming today.'

The very man who had so recently and so calmly put a pistol to his head, now became irritable.

'Enough,' he said, getting up. 'Our bet has been settled, and I consider your observations ill-timed.'

Taking up his cap, he left. His behaviour seemed to me strange and significant.

Quickly the major's rooms were cleared, and everyone went home, talking about Vulich's extraordinary behaviour. Without exception, I think, they must have styled me an egoist because I had made a bet with a man who was so fanatical a gambler that he was willing to take the chance of shooting himself in order to pouch the stakes—as if he could not have tested his fate without any intervention on my part.

I walked through the empty village streets on the way back to my quarters. The moon, full, and as red as the glare from a fire, had sur-

A FATALIST

mounted the irregular line of roofs. The stars in the dark blue firmament were shining peacefully. I laughed to think how some sages have believed the heavenly bodies to be interested in our petty disputes about areas of land or somebody's imaginary rights. Yet the luminaries, which, according to the opinion of such wiseacres, were kindled only to light our battles and our triumphs, continue to shine with unceasing splendour long after our passions and our hopes have ceased to burn, as a fire lighted at the edge of a forest by a casual traveller dies out when he has gone. Yet what strength of will these sages derived from the conviction that all heaven with its numberless inhabitants looks upon earth with a solicitude which though dumb, is unwavering.

Meanwhile we, their wretched offspring, wander over the earth without either convictions or pride, without enjoyments or fears, except for the dread which grips us at the thought of the inevitable end. We are no longer capable of great sacrifices for the welfare of mankind, or even for our own personal happiness, since we know happiness to be unattainable. We pass therefore from doubt to doubt, as our ancestors passed from delusion to delusion, but, unlike them, we are devoid of hope, lacking even the undefinable but vivid pleasure which

A FATALIST

fills the minds of those who struggle against their fellows or against fate.

Many similar thoughts flitted through my brain. I let them flow freely, having a dislike to lingering upon any particular idea. After all, to what does such concentrated meditation lead? In early youth I, also, was a dreamer, and liked to make the most of the fantasies—some gloomy, some cheerful—which chased one another through my restless, eager imagination. What remains now of all that? Nothing but weariness, like the fatigue which follows a night encounter with ghosts, and a confused memory, full of regrets. In this vain struggle I have used up the mental fire and the strength of will that are necessary for real life. I have entered upon this life when I have already lived it in imagination, with the result that it has become tedious and vile to me. I am like a man who is reading a bad imitation of a book with which he has long been familiar.

The events of the evening had made a fairly deep impression on me, and my nerves were jangled. I don't really know whether I still believe in predestination, but I firmly believed in it then. The proof seemed to me irrefutable; and though I made mock of our ancestors with their serviceable astrology, I found myself involun-

A FATALIST

tarily following their lead. But I dragged myself soon enough out of this dangerous path, and since I have made it my rule to reject nothing finally and to believe nothing blindly, I flung metaphysics aside and looked down at my feet. This precaution was opportune, for I only just escaped a fall through stumbling over something thick and soft, but obviously not alive. The road was now bathed in moonlight. I leaned forward to examine the carcass of a pig cut almost in twain by the slash of a sword. Hardly had I made out so much when I heard footsteps, and two Cossacks came running out of a lane. One of them approached me and asked whether I had seen another Cossack very drunk, chasing a pig.

'No Cossack,' I said, 'but I suppose this' (pointing to the pig) 'is the unhappy victim of his mad exploit.'

'What a brigand,' exclaimed Cossack number two. 'He's a craving for new wine, and that goes to his head. When he's screwed he wants to slash at everything he comes across. Let's go after him, Eremeich. We shall have to tie him up.'

They departed, and I went on more carefully until at length I reached my quarters.

I lodged with a Cossack sergeant, whom I

A FATALIST

liked because he was so good-tempered, but I liked his pretty daughter Nastya better still.

As usual, she was waiting for me at the back door, wrapped in furs. The moon was shining on her well-moulded lips, which were blue with cold. When she saw me, she smiled, but I was in no mood for talking to her just then. 'Goodnight, Nastya,' I said, and went straight in. Obviously she would have liked to say something, but she only sighed.

I shut the door of my room, lighted a candle, and threw myself into bed as speedily as possible. Sleep was slow of coming, but after a time I lost consciousness. Evidently, however, it had been written that I was not to have much of a night. At four in the morning two fists beat on my window. Waking with a start I shouted: 'Who's there?'

'Get up and dress,' came the reply of several voices.

I dressed quickly and went out.

'Do you know what's happened?' said three officers, all speaking together. They were pale as death.

'What?'

'Vulich has been killed.'

I was taken aback, and must have looked incredulous.

A FATALIST

'Yes, killed,' said one of them. 'We must go at once.'

'Go where?'

'We'll tell you as we go along.'

We started instantly. On the way they related what had happened, making various comments on the peculiar fate which had spared him as I had seen, to end his life half an hour afterwards. Vulich was walking alone along a dark street, when a drunken Cossack (the man who had killed the pig) rushed by. Very likely the frenzied fellow might have let Vulich alone had not the latter drawn attention to himself by calling: 'Whom are you looking for, friend?'

'For you,' answered the drunkard, brandishing his sword, and inflicting a gash in the Serb's shoulder which divided the main artery of the arm and clove Vulich almost to the heart. Death from bleeding was rapid. The two Cossacks who had met me beside the dead pig, and were hunting their mate to tie him up, saw the murder. They rushed to aid Vulich, but the victim was already at his last breath, and before he died could only murmur:

'He was right.'

I alone understood the profound significance of these words, which referred to me. I had involuntarily foretold the poor man's fate. My instinct had not misled me. His face had disclosed to me the signs of imminent death.

The murderer had barricaded himself in an unoccupied hut on the outskirts of the village. We went there. Many women were making for the same place, weeping as they walked; and now and then a belated Cossack would hurry into the street, hastily buckling on his side-arm and outrunning us. It was a scene of terrible confusion.

We arrived at length, to find a crowd surrounding the hut, whose doors and shutters were closed from within. Officers and privates were discussing what to do. Women were disputing, cursing, and wailing. Among them was an old woman with despair in her face. She was sitting on a big log, her elbows on her knees, and her head between her hands. They told me she was the murderer's mother. Her lips quivered from time to time. Was she praying or cursing?

Meanwhile something must be done to capture the criminal. But of course no one was eager to be the first to risk his life.

Going up to one of the windows, I looked through a crevice in the shutter. The Cossack, his face white as a sheet, lay on the floor, holding a pistol in his right hand. His expressive eyes

A FATALIST

were rolling frantically; occasionally he shivered and clutched his head, as though he dimly remembered what he had done. I saw little sign of determination in his restless glances, and I told the major in command that in my view it was a big mistake not to have the door broken down. Were that done some Cossacks could rush in. Better now than later, when the desperado would have fully come to his senses.

At this point an old Cossack captain went to the door and called to the man within by name. The drunkard answered: 'Here, Captain.'

'Listen, Eremeich,' said the captain. 'You've done wrong, and you know it. What can you gain by holding out? Surrender.'

'No, I won't surrender,' came the reply from within.

'Fear God,' called the captain. 'You're not an accursed heathen, but a believing Christian. If you've been tempted into a crime, you can't escape punishment, nor avoid your fate.'

'No surrender,' answered the Cossack threateningly, and I heard the click as he cocked his pistol.

'Old lady,' said the Cossack captain to the man's mother, 'come and speak to your son. Perhaps he'll listen to you. All this only angers God.

A FATALIST

Look, the officers have been kept waiting two hours.'

She looked at him and shook her head.

'Vasilii Petrovich,' said the captain to the major, 'he won't give himself up. I know him. If we break the door down, that will mean death for many of us. Would it not be better to shoot him down through that wide crack in the shutter?'

At that moment a strange thought struck me. Like Vulich I would test fate.

'Wait a minute,' I said to the major. 'I will take him alive.'

Telling the Cossack captain to start talking to the man within, I posted three privates at the door. They were to break it down and rush in to my help at a given signal. Then I went round the hut to the fateful window. My heart was beating violently.

'You accursed wretch,' the Cossack captain was shouting. 'You're laughing at us, are you? Do you think we can't finish you off?'

He began beating on the door as hard as he could. With my eyes at the crevice I was watching the movements of the Cossack, who was not expecting an attack from my side. Suddenly I tore open the shutters and rushed through the window, head down. An explosion almost deaf-

A FATALIST

ened me, and a bullet tore one of my epaulets. But the smoke which filled the room prevented my adversary from finding his sword which was lying near him. I seized his arms, the privates burst in by the door, and within three minutes the man had been bound and was taken off under guard. The crowd dispersed and the officers congratulated me—as well they might.

After such incidents, how can I help being a fatalist? And yet in matters of this kind, it is hard to know whether one is sincerely convinced or not. We often mistake for genuine assurance what is no more than the false prompting of emotion or an error of judgment. I like to have doubts about everything, but this inclination does not counteract the firmness of my character. On the contrary, I go forward more resolutely when I know what to expect. After all, there is nothing worse than death, and death is inevitable soon or late.

When I got back to the fort I told Maksim Maksimich what had happened and all that I had seen, and asked him his opinion concerning predestination. At first he did not understand what I was talking about, so I did my best to explain what the word meant. Then he said, shaking his head:

'Ah, yes, there was certainly something pecu-

A FATALIST

liar in it. You know these Asiatic pistols are apt to misfire if they're not properly oiled or if you don't press the trigger hard enough. I don't like Circassian guns either. They're unsuitable to us. The stock is so short that you can easily burn your nose on the barrel. But Circassian swords are lovely weapons.'

Having thought for a minute, he went on:

'Yes, that poor fellow Vulich had damned bad luck. But what the devil made him want to talk to a drunken Cossack at night? Certainly his fate must have been already written at the time of birth.'

I couldn't get any more out of him. He doesn't like metaphysical discussions.